ALLIE, FIRST AT LAST

BY
ANGELA CERVANTES

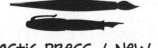

SCHOLASTIC PRESS / NEW YORK

Library of Congress Cataloging-in-Publication Data

Cervantes, Angela, author.
Allie, first at last / by Angela Cervantes.—First edition.
pages cm
Summary: Born into a family of over-achievers, fifth-grader Allie Velasco has never finished first in anything, and lately things have been going badly: her science project is ruined by a well-meaning student, her former best friend is hanging out with another girl—but now she is determined to win the Trailblazer contest with a photographic presentation about her great grandfather, the first Congressional Medal of Honor winner from their town. ISBN 978-0-545-81223-8 (hardcover)—ISBN 978-0-545-81267-2 (ebook) 1. Hispanic American families—Juvenile fiction. 2. Great-grandfathers—Juvenile fiction. 3. Contests—Juvenile fiction. 4. Self-confidence—Juvenile fiction. 5. Best friends—Juvenile fiction. 6. Elementary schools—Juvenile fiction. [1. Hispanic Americans—Fiction. 2. Great-grandfathers—Fiction. 3. Family life—Fiction. 4. Contests—Fiction. 5. Self-confidence—Fiction. 6. Best friends—Fiction. 7. Friendship—Fiction. 8. Schools—Fiction.]
I. Title.
PZ7.C3197Al 2016
813.6—dc23
[Fic]
2015031306

10 9 8 7 6 5 4 3 2 1   16 17 18 19 20

Printed in the U.S.A.   23
First edition, April 2016

Book design by Nina Goffi

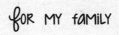
for my family

Chapter 1

Blame it on Junko Tabei. Or blame my teacher, Mrs. Wendy. She's the one who puts up a new poster of a famous person each month on our classroom wall. This month it's Junko Tabei, the first woman ever to reach the top of Mount Everest. In the poster, Junko has a pickax flung over her shoulder like she's ready to hack away at our classroom.

The month before, Mrs. Wendy hung up a poster of Neil Armstrong. Before that it was Amelia Earhart. This month Junko Tabei, pickax and all, stares me down with a challenge: When will *you* be first at something?

I know it's just a poster, but a fifth grader doesn't need that kind of pressure. It's bad enough I come from a long line of ambitious "first evers." My great-gramps, Rocky Velasco, was the first soldier EVER from our town to be awarded the Congressional Medal of Honor. He got it for being a WWII hero, but he doesn't like to talk about it. My big sister, Adriana, is the "first ever" national debate champion from our town. And that's just the tip of Mount Everest. My three siblings are first at everything and have tons of trophies and medals to show for it, but here I am about to graduate from Sendak Elementary and I haven't been first at anything.

I've had five whole years at Sendak to make my mark, and each year my rise to the top collapses like an avalanche. In first grade, we had to sell cookie dough for new playground equipment. I sold cookie dough to every single house in my neighborhood and to all the firefighters at my dad's station. Still, I came in second to Ethan Atkins, who sold a hundred tubs of cookie dough outside of church. In second grade, it was the jump-rope-a-thon for the children's hospital. I was jumping for two hours straight to beat the Sendak jump record set by Adriana. Ten minutes shy of the record, I got a leg cramp. Third grade was Sendak's math tournament. I lost in the finale to a word problem! A word problem!

I don't even want to remember my big-time fail last year. It was Sendak's annual fourth grade "Trash to Treasure" Recycling Contest. All we had to do was collect trash and make something amazing. Most kids went with the obvious and built wind chimes and bird feeders, but I took a bunch of thrown-away plastic water bottles, Styrofoam, cardboard, and empty Capri Sun packages, and made an awesome boat that actually floated! Little did I know that the black-and-white kitten we had just adopted from the animal shelter hated boats. The morning of the contest, I found Secret chewing the Styrofoam and clawing the cardboard to bits like it was made of catnip.

I've had five epic years of failure at Sendak. Today everything changes. No more failure for me! I've got a massive volcano, and I plan to be the first in my family to win Sendak Elementary School's fifth-grade science fair.

A few tables down from mine, Mr. Gribble, the head of our science department, and the other teachers stand in front of Sara Lopez's display. Mr. Gribble is asking a lot of questions, and when Sara answers, he nods and jots down notes on his clipboard. The other judges, including Mrs. Wendy, follow his lead. Sara is usually super cool and collected behind her red-rimmed glasses, but I can tell she's flustered. She fumbles with the magnets on her table and frowns.

She and I used to be best friends until Christmas break, when she decided that hanging out with Hayley Ryan was more fun.

Now she sits with Hayley at lunch and barely says a word to me. The few times I've caught her alone I've been too afraid to ask her why we're not best friends anymore. I've tried to figure out what I did wrong, but I always come up empty. Since kindergarten, I've been the coolest best friend. Last year I made her a best friend bracelet. I used her favorite color rubber bands: pink and black. Then it was her idea to invent our own secret language. She called it "best friend code." I mastered our new language in a couple of hours. Sadly, it only lasted a month, because Sara got bored with it.

Did Sara get bored with me the same way she got bored with our invented language? I glance over at her again. I bet if I win this science fair she'll realize how much she misses being my best friend. There's nothing boring about a massive volcano.

Even though I know my volcano project inside and out, I flip through my note cards. I am super prepared to answer Mr. Gribble's questions about lava, the Ring of Fire, and all the different types of volcanoes. I know more about gas bubbles than is probably legal.

Last night after dinner, I rehearsed my presentation for my family. Later, while everyone slept, I practiced in front of Secret. He eyed my volcano suspiciously and took every opportunity to whip it with his fluffy black tail. I don't think cats like volcanoes, but hopefully Mr. Gribble does. He's the one I need to convince that my project is first-prize worthy. I bet Junko Tabei faced a lot of Mr. Gribbles on her way to being the first woman to scale the tallest mountain in the world. Did it stop her?

Nope!

And it won't stop me. Mr. Gribble is the only thing that stands between me and my triumphant legacy at Sendak Elementary.

"Pssst, Alyssa! They sure are taking a long time, huh?" says Victor Garcia, the new kid at Sendak. He sidles up next to me. "I wish they'd hurry—my green slime is going to dry up and I have to pee something fierce."

I glance over at his pained face and then at his table display to the right of mine. It's the green goo project. That's so fourth grade.

"I know you're still kinda new, but only the adults call me Alyssa. Call me Allie."

"Sorry about that," he says. "Anyway, I wanted to tell

you that your volcano is super cool. Everyone says you're going to win."

"Everyone? Even Sara?" I put the note cards down on the table and watch him do the gotta-pee-so-bad shuffle. Victor transferred to Sendak after the winter break. This is the most we've ever talked.

"Yeah, everyone." He shuffles some more. "You're going to make history at Sendak for having a mega volcano."

"You'll be the one making a historic puddle if you don't go and pee already," I say.

"I can't." Victor groans. "If the judges come and I'm not here, I could be disqualified. I really need to do well at this school. It's the last year before middle school, you know."

"Well, you can't just stand here like a volcano about to lose it," I say. "If they get here while you're gone, I'll stall them at my table until you return, but hurry. Pee like you're trying to break the Guinness World Record."

"You rock, volcano girl!" He runs off.

Great. A new nickname. The only name I want is Allie, Science Fair Champion. Maybe then my big brother, Aiden, and my younger sister, Ava, will give me some respect. I'll finally make my family proud. And I can graduate from Sendak with my head held high like a true Velasco.

I rummage through my book bag to take a quick inventory. Detergent and baking soda mixture? Check. Red food dye, vinegar, and water? Check. Towels for cleanup? Check. Safety goggles for the judges? Check.

Mr. Gribble and the judges have left Sara's table. Her head is down, and she's picking at her nail polish. It's a bad habit she has whenever she's anxious. Science isn't one of Sara's favorite subjects—she's more of a musical, artsy type, but if anyone could beat me in this science fair, it would be her. She's super smart.

Which reminds me. Where is Victor? The judges are only three tables away now. I go over to his table and see that his prepared bowl of green goo is dried up. His poster board display asks *Is it a liquid or a solid?* in big, bold green print.

I poke the green ooze with my finger. No movement. "Definitely more solid," I answer. I grab his water bottle and stir a few drops into the bowl of green slime. It loosens it up. I have to give the new kid his props; it's actually very good-quality green goo, and his poster presentation is simple and fun. I like how he used stencils for the letters. I hate to admit it, but Victor's display is better than mine. Still, I have a massive volcano, and it's my golden ticket to that first-place trophy and Sendak history.

When Victor gets back, he's wiping his hands on his lab coat.

"I saved your green goo," I say. "It was dried up. I added some water."

"Thanks, volcano girl."

"Stop calling me that." I roll my eyes. I look toward Sara's table. She's folding up her display boards, which we're not supposed to do until the fair is over. I wonder if I should go over there and remind her. Maybe if I do, she'll thank me and we can start being friends again. "Hey, will you watch my table for a minute? I need to talk to Sara."

"Sure thing, volcan—Allie."

I sneak past the judges at Diego's "Tornado in a Bottle" table. Two tables away from mine. This has to be quick visit.

"Hey, Sara, what are you doing? We're supposed to keep our presentations up for when our parents and the other students arrive."

"What's the point?" She shrugs. "I'll be lucky if I place at all. My parents are going to be so disappointed." She drops her magnets into a box.

"Your parents are proud of everything you do," I say. Her parents are good friends of my parents. I know they'd never be disappointed in Sara as long as she tried hard.

8

"It was a fiasco. I wasn't prepared for the questions," Sara pouts. "Mr. Gribble is so unfair." This is classic Sara Lopez. Before every big test, she'll complain that she didn't have enough time to study. Afterward, she'll whine about how she "totally blew it." Then when the tests come back, she always has a big fat A marked on the top of the page. Sara always shrugs it off as "just luck I guess."

She's luckier than a leprechaun.

"I'm sure you did fine. You always do awesome." I hope my pep talk doesn't sound lame. I don't know why I'm so nervous all of a sudden. Sara and I were best friends for years, and now I can't speak to her like a normal human being.

"Hardly." She frowns.

I pull on my side ponytail and try to think of something to cheer her up.

I stick out my arm and show her the friendship bracelet she made from tiny turquoise and purple bands. "Look, you made me this bracelet, remember? Last year? It still hasn't fallen apart." She looks down at her magnets and doesn't say anything. Sara isn't wearing the bracelet I made her. In fact, I haven't seen her wear her bracelet since this semester started. I'm such a dork. She probably tossed it. "And you're a good songwriter. Remember that song you wrote for Secret? 'Being Fluffy Isn't Easy'? Everyone loved it."

She looks up at me from her box of magnets and frowns. "Aw, I miss Secret."

I gulp hard. She said she missed my cat and not me. I mean, I know Sara went with me and my family to pick Secret out at the animal shelter, but she could at least acknowledge that she misses me too. We've known each other since kindergarten!

Still, this is the most we've talked all semester, and I'm so happy about it that I've forgotten why I'm in the gymnasium in the first place. That is until I hear a series of whistles. I look over and see Victor whistling for me. Can't he just use his words? I have a name! Mr. Gribble and the judges have left Diego's tornado display and moved on to the table before mine.

"Hey, I've got to get back, but promise me you'll stop packing. Everyone has to see your project. It's *magnetic*." I smile. "Everyone is going to be *attracted* to it, I'm sure."

"Okay, Allie." Sara rolls her eyes, but not in a mean way. "Don't *force* me to laugh."

I know it's a long shot, but I go ahead and ask anyway. "Hey, after the science fair, my family is going to Cosmic Taco to celebrate. Do you want to come with us?"

Sara snaps two magnets together. "Celebrate what?"

My stomach churns. I could win first prize for making a fool of myself. "I mean, it's not like I'm going to win, but just in case I do win today, Mom and Dad promised me tacos. Although, I probably won't win. It's just Cosmic Tacos. Nothing fancy."

"Sure, I'll ask my parents when they get here." She smiles at me and unfolds her display board. "Good luck, Allie," she says.

"Cool. It'll be fun," I say. "Okay, later!" I rush to my table, feeling like Junko Tabei at the top of Mount Everest.

ChapteR 2

I get back to my table in plenty of time. Mr. Gribble and the judges are still hovering over Ethan's disgusting moldy bread project. How my massive volcano was assigned to be next to his table of moldy green-and-black fuzzy bread, I'll never know.

"Hey, volcano girl!" Victor rushes up to me like my neighbor's Labradoodle. Except not as cute and cuddly. "Your volcano just became a hundred times more epic!"

"Not now, Victor," I say, and wave him away. Then it hits me. What? "Wait! What did you say?" There are little green goo globs on my table. Victor is grinning from ear to ear. I want to strangle him, but Mr. Gribble and the judges are suddenly in front of me.

"Miss Alyssa Velasco," Mr. Gribble says. "This is a mighty large volcano you've created." His tone of voice makes me straighten my white lab coat. This is it. This is my chance to impress. Mrs. Wendy and the other judges huddle closer and touch my volcano. "Tell us about it."

"Of course!" I glare at Victor and flick the green goo off my table in his direction. Surely, Victor didn't put his green goo in my first-place-winning volcano. He wouldn't be that big of a goofball, would he? And if he did . . . it couldn't mess up my project, could it? I'll just up my dosage of vinegar. That's all. Trouble averted.

"Dear judges . . ." I throw my hands up like an orchestra conductor. I practiced hand gestures last night because I've seen my older sister Adriana use them at debates and it always works for her. "What you see before you today is a replica of the Guatemalan volcano known as *el volcán de Fuego*, which means, 'the Fire volcano.'" I amp up my Spanish accent when I say its name, and the judges nod approvingly. "And like *el volcán de Fuego*, my volcano is quietly waiting for just the right natural elements to come together in order to release its gaseous and destructive poison. Please stand back."

I add the premixed dish detergent and baking soda. When I look up, Sara and a few other classmates have gathered around too. "Judges, I have protective goggles for you." I pass them out, and the judges chuckle. "I don't have enough for the rest of you, so watch at your own peril."

Everyone's eyes are getting bigger, so I lengthen my words to make my presentation more dramatic. It's something I picked up from my sister Ava who is a self-proclaimed actress, but really she's just a drama queen.

"Although we don't feel it, the world's outer shell is made up of 'plates' that are always moooooving . . ." I add several drops of red dye to the vinegar. "As I speak, plates are shifting ever so sloooooowly beneath our feet. And sometimes those plates collide and there's a BOOM!" I shout.

Mr. Gribble jumps and my classmates laugh. He adjusts his glasses. "Please continue, Alyssa," he says.

"That collision causes the existing magma to rise and push through the opening of the volcano and shoot out violently, like this . . ." I pour in the vinegar. "Wait for it," I say. It should already be fizzing and erupting. I pour in more vinegar. "Okay, stand back, everyone." Still nothing. I put in more baking soda. More nothing. I stare down the throat of my volcano. Why isn't it doing something? Fizzle, please. Erupt already!

Mr. Gribble taps his pen against his clipboard, and it pounds like drums in my head. He writes a few notes. I hear every scratch of the pen against the paper. My classmates groan and move on to Victor's table. I touch my ears just to make sure hot lava isn't spewing from them.

"Um, I d-don't know what went wrong," I stammer. Mrs. Wendy comes over to me.

"It's okay, Alyssa. It was a good presentation." Mrs. Wendy pats my back and heads to Victor's green goo project.

"Don't you have any questions for me about dormant volcanoes?" I say to the judges' backs.

"We're good, thank you," Mr. Gribble says without looking back at me.

What just happened?

"Are you okay, Allie?" Sara asks.

"I don't understand," I mumble. "I added enough baking soda and vinegar to erupt a dozen volcanoes." I pause to retrace my steps. "You know, when I came back, Victor said something about my volcano being more epic. And there was green goo on my table . . ."

Sara's eyebrows rise. "Not good."

"I thought, no way could he . . . but . . ." I take a long plastic spoon from my backpack and start digging into the mouth of my volcano with it. When I pull it out, there are traces of baking soda mixed with wet globs of detergent. All of that looks normal. It should have worked.

Victor is deep into his presentation about the mixing of chemicals to create blah blah blah. After a few seconds, everyone is oohing and aahing over the fresh batch of green slime he's made. My volcano should have erupted. Everyone should be oohing and aahing over *my* science project. Not his!

The only way to know what went wrong is to see inside. I dig my nails deep into the clay and try to pull away chunks, but it's caked on hard. Have to admit, I did a great job on the clay. I could really use Junko's pickax right now.

"I have to get in there," I grunt, and I tip the wooden platform of my volcano onto the table.

"What are you doing, Allie?" Sara says.

Clumps of green slime, vinegar, baking soda, and dish detergent dribble from the volcano onto the table and floor. I scoop up a clumpy glob of green goo. My perfectly measured ingredients should have mixed and turned into an epic lava. Instead it looks like an outtake from an old sci-fi movie. Green goo has killed my volcano. My chance to win the science fair at Sendak has been slimed!

Chapter 3

"Allie, that's what I was trying to tell you," Victor says. "I thought it'd be cool if the volcano had some gooey lava dribbling outside of it. I didn't think it would ruin it."

"Yes, because that makes so much sense. A volcano dribbling green slime!" I hiss. "He admits the sabotage!" I point at Victor and look to Mr. Gribble and Mrs. Wendy for swift punishment. Both of them are shaking their heads in disbelief. Victor steps back.

"Victor, why would you touch another student's project?"

Mrs. Wendy asks a little too nicely for me. She should be furious. I'm furious. Now is the time for being furious.

"I didn't mean it in a bad way. I really thought it'd be cool. I thought you'd like it, Allie."

"Like it? Do you think Junko Tabei would have liked an avalanche as she climbed Mount Everest?"

"Junko what?"

"Don't play dumb, Victor." I glare at him. Just then, the gymnasium doors open, and parents and students arrive.

"You helped me with my project. You added more water to my green slime, and I just wanted to help you."

"You added more water to his project?" Mrs. Wendy asks. The way she says this reminds me of traffic lights signaling drivers to proceed with caution. It's a yellow-light question.

"Just a little bit." I shrug. "While he went to the bathroom."

"Okay, students, that's enough." Mr. Gribble holds up his hands. "Parents are here, and I am officially closing the science fair competition. I think we've seen and definitely heard everything we need to hear." He turns to Victor. "Victor, you're disqualified. Pack up your stuff."

Victor's head drops. I don't feel sorry for him one bit.

"What about me?" I ask.

Mr. Gribble gazes over my tipped volcano and soaked table. "Allie, you should clean up."

"What about my project? It would have erupted if Green-Goo Garcia over there hadn't messed with it."

"But, Allie . . ." Mrs. Wendy starts. "You left your table, right?"

"Well, yes, but that was just a quick run to cheer up Sara," I say. "She was sad." Surely, they wouldn't hold that against me. "I was only gone for a minute. I was here before you even noticed."

Mrs. Wendy looks over at Sara's table. Sara's parents have arrived, and she's all smiles showing off her magnets.

"She seems to be doing fine."

"Well, sure, *now* she's fine, but you should have seen her—"

"Sorry, Allie, but if you had stayed at your table as everyone was instructed to do, Victor wouldn't have had the opportunity to mess with your project," Mr. Gribble says. My face feels suddenly hot. "And your volcano would have worked as you intended. You're not disqualified, but you've lost points. Take it as a lesson learned."

"But Sara was packing up her stuff . . ."

Mr. Gribble and the judges walk off toward the podium and the trophy table. I watch them take a seat and share notes.

"You see that, Victor?" I snarl as I pull paper towels out of my bag. "They're counting scores for the best project, which should be mine."

"I said I was sorry . . ."

"Don't talk to me," I mutter. Victor is packing his stuff into a cardboard box, when his family arrives. It's a regular Garcia family reunion: his mom, dad, grandparents, and four younger brothers and sisters jump around him like he's the ice cream truck. His father in crisp-ironed jeans, black shirt, cowboy boots, and hat, picks up some of the green slime, laughs, and pats Victor on the back. *"Mi hijo, el futuro científico!"* I feel a little bad when Victor lowers and shakes his head and says, "I have a long way to go to be a scientist."

Although they are mostly speaking Spanish and I don't always understand everything, I hear Victor squeak out the whole story and mention me. His father's voice is suddenly deeper. He's giving Victor a good talking-to in Spanish. When they see me watching, all of them become silent, and they look at me with sad, apologetic eyes. I turn back to my table and do my best to wipe up vinegar and baking soda.

"Allie?" Victor walks over to me with his hands in his lab coat pockets. His family follows behind. "We're leaving now. I just wanted to say I'm sorry again. I feel really bad." His entire family nods. Just a few minutes ago, they were laughing, playing with green goo, calling him a scientist. They were so proud. Now, not so much. My chest aches.

"My son is very sorry," his mom says with a thick Spanish accent. She gives me a warm hug and then takes the paper towels from my hands and cleans up the floor where vinegar spilled. Then his grandma hugs me and picks globs of clay and slime off my lab coat. His grandpa makes apologies in Spanish for Victor. His kind smile reminds me of my *bisabuelo*, my great-grandpa. I wish he were here right now. If he were, he'd put his arm around me and tell me everything will be all right.

I think the lovefest is over, when Victor's four brothers and sisters mob me with hugs. His toddler-age sister holds my hand and tells me I'm "pretty." Finally, Victor's father shoos the children away from me with his cowboy hat.

"Please forgive our son for ruining your project," he says. "You worked very hard. We raised him better than that. *Lo siento mucho.*"

I bite my lip. I know I should smile and say I forgive Victor, but it's so hard. What about me? It was my chance to be a champion. It was my last chance to make my mark at Sendak before I graduate. I glance toward the trophy table, and then back at Victor. He's removed his lab coat, and it's wadded up in his hands.

I read online that Junko almost died when she climbed Mount Everest. While camping, she and her guides were blindsided by an avalanche. Even though they were buried in snow, they still survived, and a few days later, she reached the top. I think about what Junko Tabei would do at a moment like this. From everything I read about her, she seems like a humble, kind, and determined woman. Junko would find another way to climb again.

"It's okay, Victor," I finally say.

Then the hugs start all over. Victor is smiling, and his father pats him on the head. "See, she is a nice girl. She forgives you. You are lucky," his father says. This makes me smile.

"Thanks, Allie," Victor says. We shake hands. Victor and his family leave as loudly as they arrived. As they exit, my parents and three siblings approach.

The closer my family gets to my display, the more my palms sweat. I wipe them against my lab coat, but it's no use. I was supposed to be the first Velasco to win the Sendak Science Contest. When they're finally in front of what's left of my volcano, their mouths gape at the mess. Even Adriana, my favorite sister, can't hide her shock. Aiden whistles like a torpedo has been launched and I'm the target. Instead of an explosion, I get Ava. She steps forward in her purple soccer uniform and shakes her head.

"Looks like no celebration dinner tonight."

Chapter 4

At our house, we have a bookcase in the living room filled with glassed-etched awards, towering gold-plated trophies, and a slew of silver and gold medals with colorful ribbons that my family has won. It's the trophy shelf.

The largest trophy on the shelf belongs to Adriana. She won the national high school debate championship last year. She traveled all the way to Miami and argued her way to the top until all her competitors were argued out. All of us flew down to Miami to be with her, and I got chills when my sister held the giant gold trophy over her head. She held it the same way Sara is hoisting the first-place science fair trophy over her head right now. She won with the magnet project. The crowd of parents, teachers, and students is going wild with applause for her.

Although my parents have chosen to abandon me and stand with Sara's parents at her winning magnet display, Adriana hasn't left my side. She puts her arm around my shoulders and gives me a squeeze.

"Try to be happy for Sara," she whispers to me. That's when I realize my arms are crossed and I'm pouting. Ava and Aiden are up in the bleachers on their phones texting and cackling. I'm pretty sure they're sending snarky texts about me. They always do. When Ava notices me looking, she sticks her tongue out like the eight-year-old reptile she is.

"Ignore her." Adriana rolls her eyes. "She just got another commercial deal. We found out before we got here. She's been nonstop unbearable. More than usual."

"Another commercial?" I ask. Ava already has a recurring commercial gig with a local used-car dealership. The owner wears a big Mexican sombrero and yells things like "No money down!" and "These deals won't last long!" At the end of every commercial, he points at the camera and shouts, "Are you going to buy your next car from Sifuentes Auto Mart?" That's Ava's cue. The camera pans to her sitting in a pink convertible, wearing a pink dress and a big pink smile. She throws up her fist and shouts, "*Sí* for Sifuentes Auto Mart!" She's been doing commercials for Mr. Sifuentes since she was four years old. When we're out grocery shopping or at one of Aiden's soccer games, people fawn all over her. They tell her how cute she is and how she'll be a big movie star someday.

Adriana sighs. "This time, she'll be doing commercials for the new water park. Part of her contract includes free passes whenever she wants."

"Free passes?" I shriek. I would love to have free passes to the new water park. I wonder if the passes include family members. I hope so.

"We should be happy for . . ." Adriana's phone beeps. She looks at the incoming text and then glares up at Ava and Aiden on the bleachers. I lean in to see the text and manage to glimpse my name and *loser* before Adriana deletes it. "It's nothing. Like I said, we should be happy for her, but she makes it impossible."

I am so doomed. Adriana is leaving for college next year. Her junior year, she announced to the entire family that she was only applying to Ivy League schools, which made me itch because anything with ivy in it can't be good. Last summer, I had a nasty case of poison ivy and had to put socks on my hands to keep me from scratching. Adriana will be the first in our family to go to an Ivy League school. And I'll be at home left to deal with Aiden and Ava on my own.

"C'mon, let's go congratulate Sara," she says, and loops arms with me.

With every step, I think of what I'll say to Sara. I don't want to sound like the dork that lost the science fair. I need to be cool. I should act like it doesn't bother me. I should be happy for her. I could really use some of Ava's acting skills right now.

When we approach, Sara's parents immediately hug me.

"Allie, we never see you anymore!" her mom exclaims, and gives me a hug. I want to tell her it's because Sara barely talks to me, but I just smile. She runs her hands over my hair. "I love your side ponytail."

"Thanks, Mrs. Lopez."

"Sara told us what happened with your volcano. What a mess," Mr. Lopez says.

"Oh," I say. I'm stunned at how fast Sara has told her parents. I bet she's probably texted the whole school about it. At Sendak Elementary, gossip doesn't spread like burning lava—it flies like a tornado. Somehow, I always forget that. "It's okay. I'm happy Sara won."

"You're a good friend." Mrs. Lopez pats my head.

"She's one in a million," my dad says, and pulls on my ponytail, which annoys me. "But she puts too much pressure on herself." Sara's parents look sympathetic, and I want to hide under the nearest table. "And like Bon Jovi sings, 'It doesn't make a difference if we make it or not. We've got each other and that's a lot for love.'" My dad is always quoting '80s music. Mr. and Mrs. Lopez laugh, but I wish they wouldn't. It only encourages him.

"No, I don't," I mumble. Before he can respond with more wisdom from the '80s, I escape to where Sara is talking to a few of our classmates. She has the first-place trophy tucked under her arm. If that were my trophy, I wouldn't stick it in my armpit. I'd polish it every night. That prize would be the shiniest award on our family trophy shelf.

When Sara sees me, she pulls me next to her.

"Allie, what happened? Did Victor get in trouble?" she asks. Then she looks around at all the other students. "Victor totally sabotaged her volcano." Everyone shakes their heads. "He should be kicked out of school."

Sara's reaction takes me aback. It was my project that was ruined. Not hers. She won. Why is she so bothered? Maybe she's feeling loyal to me? That's definitely a good sign that maybe we're friends again. Still, it's harsh saying Victor should be kicked out of Sendak. He just got here.

"He apologized," I answer. "In fact his entire family apologized. It was sweet—"

"I saw his family when they arrived," Hayley speaks up. I hadn't noticed her before, but of course she'd be there. These days, she and Sara are always together. She tosses her long brown hair behind her shoulder. "They were dressed up like they were going to a rodeo, not a science fair. Did you see the hat and boots his father was wearing?" Hayley does a little rodeo dance. "We're here to round up the green goo!" she jokes. Everyone laughs, including Sara, which surprises me. Why would she laugh at that? Why is that even funny?

"Well, anyway, good job, Sara," I say, trying to change the subject. The whole conversation makes me uncomfortable. "Congrats."

Adriana comes over and drapes her arm around my shoulders. "Say your good-byes. Mom and Dad are ready to go." All my classmates gasp in awe. My big sister is a rock star to my classmates. Even Hayley steps back shyly. This makes me feel better. When Adriana was at Sendak Elementary, she made history by being the first Sendak student to win the Mayor's Youth Power Award for the It Takes a Village tutoring program she started. Usually it's awarded to middle and high school students, but she won it her last year at Sendak. And if that wasn't enough, she's also fashion-magazine beautiful. Her picture, along with a few other notable Sendak alums, is up on the wall in the school office.

"Are we still going to Cosmic Taco?" I ask.

"Of course!" Adriana smiles.

"Sara . . ." I start. Hayley locks arms with Sara and pulls her closer like they're both magnets, which stops me cold. I press on. "Did you still want to go for tacos?"

"Oh, I didn't realize you guys were still going," she says coolly. "Hayley invited me to get pizza and since you didn't win . . . I mean . . . I'm sorry, I just figured the whole Cosmic Taco thing wasn't happening. I'm going with Hayley's family now."

Ouch. Could this day get any worse? I want to say something, but if I open my mouth, I'll bawl.

"Thanks, though," Sara adds.

I look up at Adriana for strength.

"No problem," Adriana says with a big smile. "We'll go together another time." Adriana takes me by the elbow, and we zoom away. Adriana should really wear a cape. She saves me all the time.

ChAPTER 5

We go out to eat, but we don't end up at Cosmic Taco. When I didn't win the science fair, Ava made reservations at her favorite Italian restaurant. And my parents always go along with whatever the future movie star, Ava Velasco, wants. After all, she is going to be famous. More famous than Junko Tabei. More famous than our great-grandpa. More famous than I'll ever dream to be.

When we're seated at the table, Adriana takes a chair next to me and pushes the menu away from her.

"Mom and Dad, I don't think this is fair to Allie. So in protest, I will only be having a glass of water."

I gulp hard. Sure, I wanted Cosmic Taco more than anyone, but I hope that doesn't mean I am supposed to refuse to eat too. Today has already been lousy. Plus, I'm really hungry and can't resist melted-cheesy breadsticks.

"Don't be angry, Adriana," says Dad, all matter-of-fact. "The deal was that if Allie won, we'd go to Cosmic Taco to celebrate, but things changed and Ava was begging for Italian." He opens a menu to deflect Adriana's cold stare. The waiter brings glasses of water and a basket of warm breadsticks.

"I told everyone, even Sara, that we were going to Cosmic Taco," I say. It comes out like a big, fat gripe, and Aiden looks up from his phone to scoff.

"Who ordered the whine?" he says. I shrink into my chair. Why do I even open my mouth?

"Hey, watch it!" Adriana points a fork at him. Ever since Aiden made the All-Star city soccer team this year, he's been a snot. He's the youngest to be recruited for the team. He has the newspaper announcement pinned up on his wall surrounded by posters of his favorite soccer players. Someday, I'm sure he'll be on a poster in some kid's room. He's that good.

Mom follows with a stern look for Aiden and then turns her gaze to me. "Look, Allie. Honey Bear." She smiles and uses her and dad's little nickname for me. The truth is, I turn to mush when she smiles at me, and I'm not the only one. Her smile is the reason she is the number one news anchor in Kansas City. "It can't be all about you . . ." she starts. I bite down on my bottom lip and try to remember when there was ever a day devoted entirely to me. Maybe the day I was born? "You know that Ava signed a new commercial contract today. It's very exciting." She winks at Ava. "You're her big sister. You can handle it. What's the harm, anyway? You love Italian Gardens." She grabs the basket of breadsticks and passes it to Aiden.

I don't even get first dibs. This day just keeps getting better.

"What's the harm?" Adriana pounds the table with her fist. "You promised her last night in the dining room. All of us were there. You and dad said to her—"

"Adriana, please." My mom puts her hands up. "This is not the debate championship, okay?"

"Whatever," Adriana says.

"Yeah, whatever," I repeat like a deranged parrot, but it's all I can manage.

"If Adriana isn't eating, can I have her breadstick?" Aiden asks.

"Don't be greedy," Dad warns. "Adriana is going to eat. She can't resist a tasty cheesy-garlicky bread stick, no?" My dad says this in a goofy way that usually makes Adriana laugh, but today it doesn't. She narrows her eyes at him.

"It's not right, Dad."

"See, she's not going to eat one." Aiden takes an extra breadstick and smirks. "I need the carbs for the game tomorrow. Someone in this family needs to win this week."

"Oh, snap!" Ava chirps.

"None of that." Mom wags her finger at him.

"You're turning into a real—" Adriana starts at Aiden, but stops when a few voices loudly and happily greet someone. She gives Aiden an I'll-get-you-later look. Ava and Aiden stash away their phones. The change in everyone can only mean one thing—my *bisabuelo* has arrived.

He walks into the dining area wearing his usual jeans, button-down shirt, and navy blue Veterans of Foreign Wars baseball cap and jacket. As he walks toward us, he smiles wide and shakes hands with the restaurant staff. Everyone knows my *bisabuelo*. He is the only living World War II Medal of Honor recipient in our state. A year ago, a local filmmaker made a documentary about him. It showed at all the fancy film festivals in the country and at most of the theaters in town. Now we can't go anywhere with Great-Gramps without someone recognizing him. Perfect strangers, usually other war veterans, write him and invite him to coffee. My great-grandpa says he hasn't had to buy his own cup of joe since that documentary came out. I think it's funny that he calls coffee "joe."

Anyway, the award is a huge deal. He won it by taking down a whole Nazi machine-gun nest and rescuing a bunch of wounded soldiers. Still, he doesn't show off the medal. He says it's buried in a box in the basement. My mom and dad nag at him to display it on the trophy shelf, but he won't do it.

One by one, Great-Gramps goes around the table to kiss all of us. "What happened to Cosmic Taco?" he asks as he takes a seat at the head of the table. The waiter fills his glass with water and places a fresh batch of breadsticks in front of him. "I was on my way there when I got the message. It's not your favorite place anymore, Allie?"

"Yeah, Dad, explain why we're here," Adriana says. She crosses her arms and leans back in the chair.

"Well, this is the thing . . ." Dad clears his throat. "The science fair didn't turn out the way we hoped for Allie, but the good news is that Ava signed a contract to appear in a new commercial, so we let her choose the restaurant."

After a pause, Great-Gramps tips his hat to Ava. "Congrats to you, Ava."

My tummy flip-flops. I stare down at the list of pastas on the menu, knowing that I won't have the stomach to eat a thing now. Not even a cheesy breadstick.

"Allie," Great-Gramps calls out to me. "*Ven aquí, mija.*"

I go over and face him. This is a million times worse than Mr. Gribble judging me. I don't ever want to disappoint Bisabuelo.

"What happened today at the science fair? Did you do your best?" he asks.

"I did my best, Bisa," I say. I should probably tell him the whole story about the green goo and about Victor Garcia, but I can't. I don't know why. It would just be an excuse. "It just wasn't my day."

"It wasn't your day, eh?" He takes my hands and pats them. "Well, I know a little something about that. Help me up." I help him stand. "*Vamos.* Let's go."

"What? We just got here," my father says. "Where are you going?"

"We're going to Allie's favorite place." He gives my hand an extra squeeze. I feel so happy I want to cry. Next thing I know, Adriana is at my side too.

"I'm going with you guys." She drapes her arm around my shoulders. "See? Great-Gramps gets it."

"But, Abuelo . . ." my father says.

Great-Gramps turns to him. "Look, if the rest of you want to join me, volcano-expert Allie, and the lovely Adriana at Cosmic Taco, you're most welcome to do so. We're going to celebrate Allie's performance at the science fair like we promised. Win or lose, she worked hard and deserves a cosmic taco."

"But, Bisabuelo, I signed a contract today," Ava says while pulling out her phone to show him a photo. "See, it's a new contract for the new water park. I'm going to be famous like you."

Great-Gramps gives her a gentle smile. "Avita, I'm proud of you too, and I don't doubt for a second that you'll be more famous than me, but today was promised to Allie. We gave her our word. And in life, your word is your character."

"But . . ." Ava puts her phone down on the table. "I wanted raviolis."

"I've already eaten like two breadsticks," says Aiden. "Won't it be wrong to leave now?"

"You decide what's right, *mi familia*." Great-Gramps nods to my father and then turns to head out of the dining room. Adriana and I follow him. We stop at the bar, and Great-Gramps expresses his regrets to the owner for leaving so abruptly. Mr. Grimaldi doesn't blink. He asks Bisabuelo to wait a second and then rushes back to the kitchen. While we wait, I look back at the table. Mom and Dad look confused. Ava and Aiden are on their phones again. I've let my family down, and now we're not eating dinner together.

"Don't worry, Allie." Great-Gramps puts his arm around my shoulders. "They'll meet us at Cosmic Taco." I feel a little better after he says that. I wrap my arms around his waist and hug him tight. On the wall behind the bar, there are framed black-and-white photos of famous Italian Americans. This is the first time I've had the chance to really look at the photos. Most of them are baseball players, but there are also few famous singers and actors that I've heard my *bisabuelo* mention. A boxer holds up a championship belt. A beautiful actress clutches a trophy. A famous singer holds just a microphone. Maybe he's like me and has never won a trophy.

"Bisa, did that singer in that picture ever win a trophy?"

"Old blue eyes, there?" Bisa smiles. "He was a double threat. He won awards for his singing and acting." Bisa starts humming a song I don't know and twirls me. I think it'd be cool to be so admired that a restaurant would put a picture up of you on their wall. Would anyone ever put a picture of me up on a library, classroom, or restaurant wall?

When Mr. Grimaldi returns, he presents my great-gramps with a large slice of tiramisu in a to-go box. "It's always an honor to have you in our restaurant," he says. "Please return soon, my friend."

Inside Bisabuelo's car, I hold the box of tiramisu on my lap. It's a clear box tied up with a red ribbon. What do I have to do to get free tiramisu in a cute little box with a pretty ribbon? My great-gramps had to fight in a war and save lives. There's no way I can compete.

Still, I can't help but think if I had won today, everything would be different. All of us would be happy together at Cosmic Taco . . . even Sara would be with us. The science fair trophy would be placed at the center of the table, and we'd be talking about how I've made my mark at Sendak. Finally.

As we drive away, I glance back toward Italian Gardens. My parents, Ava, and Aiden, with their heads down, leave the restaurant and walk to the car. They'll meet us at Cosmic Taco just as my great-gramps said they would, but they're not doing it for me.

CHAPTER 6

We are regulars at Cosmic Taco, so the minute we walk through the bright turquoise door, Cesar, our favorite waiter, sits us at our special table. It's a comfy corner booth, but the best thing about this table is that it has a little old-fashioned jukebox on the wall that plays Mexican songs. Great-Gramps loves it.

"Where's the rest of the *familia*?" Cesar asks as he passes out menus, which we don't really need because we know it by heart.

"They're on their way." Great-Gramps smiles. Cesar leaves to get us a pitcher of *horchata*, a milky rice drink flavored with cinnamon. It's my favorite. Great-Gramps digs into his wallet and gives Adriana a few dollar bills to feed the jukebox.

"Chente?" Adriana asks him, using the nickname of the famous Mexican singer, Vicente Fernández.

Bisabuelo closes his eyes like he's thinking about a song. "In honor of strong young women, let's hear Lola Beltrán."

"You got it." Adriana inserts dollars and selects all of Great-Gramp's favorite songs. The first song is "*Cucurrucucú paloma.*" It's a depressing song about lost love, but it doesn't have a sad affect on Great-Gramps or Adriana. In between sips of *horchata*, they sing along, smiling at each other, "*Ay, ay, ay, ay, ay, cantaba.*"

Great-Gramps loves this place as much as I do because everything about Cosmic Taco breathes life and history. The entire interior wall is a mural of famous Mexican movie stars from the '30s and '40s sitting at a long table in their suits and evening gowns eating tacos. The glamorous starlet María Félix sits next to the beautiful Dolores del Río, and they each hold a soft taco in a long-gloved hand. Cantinflas, the legendary comic, holds up a crispy taco while the actor Anthony

Quinn has a puffy fried flour taco on his plate. Between the Mexican movie stars on the walls, Lola's voice booming in the background, and the spicy aroma rising from the kitchen, Cosmic Taco transports me to a different world. A world where volcanoes aren't ruined with green slime, best friends don't stop talking to you, and there's a trophy on the family shelf with my name on it.

Great-Gramps calls out to Cesar for a large order of guacamole and chips. "Aiden and Ava can't be mad if they see guacamole when they get here, eh?"

"Good strategy." Adriana winks.

All of sudden, my *bisabuelo* starts coughing. Adriana reaches across to hand him a napkin. His entire body shakes as he coughs into the napkin. He's been having these coughing fits more lately. When it starts, I turn away. I feel ashamed that I'm not more like Adriana and I don't try to help him. When he coughs low and hard like that, I can't watch. It scares me and I freeze up. Cesar rushes over, concerned. Bisabuelo collects himself and thanks him. Great-Gramps manages a weak smile at me. I exhale.

"Bisabuelo, have you been to the doctor?" I ask.

"Many times, but there's nothing they can do when you're just old."

"You're not old, Bisabuelo," Adriana says.

"In my *corazón* no, but my lungs and my bones are ninety-one years old. I'm *viejo*."

He reaches for us across the table and pats our hands. "I'm lucky to have such sweet girls worry about me, but I'm fine." He leans back against the booth. "When I was your age, I wasn't nearly as sweet as you two."

Adriana shakes her head. "Bisabuelo, at my age you were fighting in Europe and saving lives. I haven't saved anyone."

He winces. "That's not true, *mija*. What you do with your tutoring program is important. You're saving lives by giving those children an opportunity to have a future."

"Totally," I say. The tutoring program that Adriana started at Sendak helps children that need extra help with school but can't afford tutors. She still oversees the program, but has actual staff and volunteers to help run it now.

"Maybe . . ." she says. Cesar places a basket of chips and a bowl of guacamole in front of her. "Still, I'm no hero like you, Bisabuelo."

"If it were up to me," says Great-Gramps, "those documentary producers would have made a movie about you two instead."

"A documentary about me would be big-time boring," I say. "I haven't won or done anything."

"You're a great little sister. That's something," Adriana says. I smile at her because it's nice to hear, but not enough.

"You're still so young, *mija*. You are just learning how to make your way through the world. Be patient with yourself," says Great-Gramps.

"But Adriana and Aiden won awards and scholarships at Sendak at my age. Ava is already a theater legend at Sendak, and she's a year younger than me. It's like everyone in this family is on their way to the top of Mount Everest and I'm stuck at base camp. And if the science fair is any indication of how the rest of my life will go, it's going to be one big slimy mess."

"What happened exactly?" Adriana asks.

"I was at my table with my glorious *volcán de Fuego*, but I left to talk to Sara because she seemed sad and was taking her display down. I walked away for just a minute—" Adriana raises her eyebrows at me. "I know. I should have never left my volcano. What was I thinking? I know."

"You went to cheer up Sara?" Adriana asks. I bite down on my lip. I always do that when I feel embarrassed. "That's not bad, Allie. That's being a good friend."

"Yes, except that I lost the science fair because one of my classmates . . . well, it's complicated."

"You went to make a friend feel better, to help her out. I'm proud of you," Bisa says.

"Me too," says Adriana.

"You don't understand. Because of that, I lost. Once again, I have nothing for the trophy shelf."

"*Mija*, the best rewards in life don't fit on a shelf," Bisabuelo says.

I slump down in the booth. "You always tell me that, but I'm tired of everyone else winning trophies, medals, and pretty shiny things. Sara doesn't even care. She won, took her trophy, and went for pizza with Hayley."

Speaking of pretty shiny things, the door of Cosmic Taco swings open. The rest of my family rushes in. Bisa said they'd come. He was right.

Aiden slides into the booth beside Great-Gramps. Ava scoots in next to me. She gives me a quick smile as she grabs a chip from the basket and scoops up guacamole.

"Oh, this is yummy," she says.

"So glad you guys are here," I say. It sounds dorky, but I really do mean it. I was worried that Aiden and Ava would be pouty, but so far they're focused on the chips and guac.

"We're glad to be here, Honey Bear," my dad says. Mom

leans across to give me a peck on the cheek before sliding into the booth. Dad sits next to Aiden and nudges him. "What did we talk about in the car?"

Aiden puts down the chip on its way to his mouth. "Oh, yeah . . ." He exchanges a glance with Ava.

"Right," she says. "I'll go first." She shifts to face me in the booth and bites down on her lip as if whatever she's about to say is painful. She truly is a great actress. "Allie, I'm sorry for being mean to you. I'm going to respect you like Dad says I should because you're my older sister. Older people should be respected."

"Okay . . . thanks, Ava," I say. "I'm only fourteen months older than you, by the way."

"I'm sorry about the whole winning comment," Aiden says. "It was rude. You're my little sister and you're trying your best, so I should support you more."

"Wow. Thanks, Aiden."

"Bravo." Bisabuelo tips his glass of *horchata* at both of them. "Good job."

"See?" Mom says, and smiles. "Everyone's happy. Let's eat."

Cesar comes over and asks us if we're ready to order.

"Yes, I'm hungry like the wolf," my dad adds, and we all groan because once he gets started on the '80s songs, it

46

doesn't end, but I don't mind tonight. We're all together munching on guacamole and the science fair fiasco is over.

"Ava and Allie, *mis estrellas* . . ." Great-Gramps calls out to us. "See that beautiful starlet behind you?"

We glance back at the mural, where a red-lipped, dark-eyed movie star stands tall with her crispy taco.

"Yes, it's Katy Jurado, the Mexican actress. You've told us before," says Ava.

"Yes, but did I tell you that she was the first Mexican actress to be nominated for an Academy Award for acting?"

"Really?" Ava turns again and this time gazes longer at Katy Jurado like she's measuring her up. "I didn't know that."

After a few minutes, Ava leans in and whispers to me. "Old Katy up there may be the first Mexican actress to be nominated, but I'm going to be the first Mexican American to *win* a lead actress Oscar."

Her confidence hits me like an avalanche.

"It's *my* destiny. I'll be the first." She takes a sip of *horchata*.

Where did Ava get so much confidence? Were they giving it away at Sendak on a day I was home sick? Was there a sale on it at our favorite store and I missed it?

At the science fair, I was sure that I would win. I also thought that Sara and I would be eating tacos together right now, like the best friends we used to be. Instead, I didn't win the first-place trophy. I have no best friend. And I still have no idea how I'll make my mark before I graduate from Sendak Elementary this year. Confidence level is zero.

Chapter 7

Back at school on Monday, Junko Tabei and her pickax are no longer on our classroom wall. She's been replaced with the poet Gwendolyn Brooks. I don't even put my book bag down at my desk. I study the new poster while my classmates file in past me and take their seats.

In the poster, Gwendolyn Brooks is reading from a book. It's as if someone snuck up on her at the library and snapped a picture. I bet she didn't know that years later that picture would be made into a poster and pinned up on our fifth-grade classroom wall. Under her image it says her name in bold letters and *The first African American writer to win the Pulitzer Prize.*

"Mrs. Wendy," I call out as she's writing on the board. "What happened to the other poster? The one with Junko Tabei? Usually you keep the poster up for a whole month."

Mrs. Wendy comes over. "Way to pay attention, Alyssa," she says, and pats my head like I'm her pet poodle. "Since it's almost April, National Poetry Month, I thought I'd go ahead and switch it to feature a poet."

"What's the Pulitzer Prize?"

"It's a prize awarded every year to the best American writers, poets, and musicians."

"Did she get a fancy medal?"

"Oh, I'm sure of it. The Pulitzer is a big deal."

"A big deal, huh?" The bell rings, and I take my seat in the third row behind Grace Lentz and in front of Diego O'Brien. I rummage through my book bag for my notebook and favorite pen. From the corner of my eye, I see Sara chatting with Hayley. No surprise. Victor waves at me the way people wave from parade floats—nonstop and with a big goofy grin. I shift my gaze to the blackboard but I don't want to be rude, so I wave back at him really fast.

"Before we start today, I want to recognize our science fair winners," says Mrs. Wendy.

"Diego, Sara, Ethan, will you stand up?" I turn around in my seat to watch them stand while the entire class claps. I thought I was over it, but I get a lump in my throat. It hurts when I think of how close I came to winning. I'd been working on my project since January, and now it's nearly April. The school year is over in two months, and with it my chance to make my mark at Sendak. How did I let this happen?

"Okay, let's get out your notebooks. You'll want to take notes," says Mrs. Wendy. "Alyssa made a great observation this morning. She noticed the poster of the great poet Gwendolyn Brooks on the wall."

I turn ever so slightly to see if Sara has reacted to the mention of my name, but she is pulling something out of her desk.

"The reason I posted this is because it's almost April, and if you recall, the deadline for the Kansas Trailblazer Contest is coming up. So far, I've heard of only two of you entering. I think Sendak can do better than that. What do you think? You can submit an original poem, song, or photo essay. Each of you should try for it."

Not happening. I'm more of a science-fizz-bam-boom-poof girl than an artsy-fartsy type.

"Remember, there's extra credit if you submit for the contest," Mrs. Wendy announces in a singsongy voice.

Still not happening, no matter how singsongy she makes it sound. She brought this Trailblazer contest up right after winter break, and I wasn't interested then and I'm not interested now.

"How much extra credit?" Victor asks.

"An extra ten points toward your final English grade," says Mrs. Wendy. Some of the kids clap. I open my notebook to a fresh blank page. At the top, I write *Allie's List of Firsts.* After the science fair fiasco, it's time for me to get serious about my destiny. If I don't do something amazing this year to make my mark, I just don't deserve the Velasco name. I need something fast. Something epic.

"Poetry and songwriting are great ways to express yourself because they reveal truth and beauty . . ." Mrs. Wendy's voice rises and her hands float in front of her. I look around the classroom to see if anyone is interested in revealing truth and beauty. Sara is cleaning her glasses. Hayley is putting on lip gloss. Victor sits forward like he's listening hard to Mrs. Wendy, but I bet he's daydreaming about green goo. "And photography isn't just a bunch of selfies. Photography is images captured in a second that breathe and burn forever."

Burn forever? Sounds dangerous. No thank you.

"Is the extra credit only if we win the contest?" Victor asks.

Geesh! He must really need the extra credit. Poor guy.

"Ten points for entering. If someone from my class wins the whole thing, that would be fantastic!" She beams. "I'll give that student even more points toward their English final grade. How's that?"

Victor seems pleased and writes something down in his notebook.

"Think about this, class . . ." Mrs. Wendy continues. "Despite our academic reputation as one of the best schools in the city, there's never been a winner from Sendak."

Never been a winner from Sendak? How's that possible? I raise my hand.

"Mrs. Wendy, are you sure there's never been a winner from Sendak?" I ask.

"Yes, I'm one hundred percent certain."

She has my attention now. I raise my hand again.

"So if someone from Sendak won, he or she would be the first ever?" I ask. Hayley snorts, but I ignore it because I've heard all her judgmental snorts, sarcastic grunts, and dismissive scoffs and it doesn't bother me anymore. In fact, I think she should see a veterinarian about all these animal noises she makes.

"Yes. First ever. Isn't that exciting?" Mrs. Wendy knows she has me now.

There are murmurs rising from the classroom and several hands pop up.

"Yes, Diego?" Mrs. Wendy asks.

"So it has to be like a famous person who was first at something?" Diego asks.

"It doesn't have to be a famous person necessarily. Trailblazers can be anyone. The original trailblazers were American settlers who traveled west for a better life. It just has to be someone who tried something different in order to make life better for others."

Grace raises her hand, and Mrs. Wendy calls on her.

"I've already started a poem for my mom, but can I submit a song too?" Grace asks.

"Overambitious much?" Hayley says, and I look back to glare at her. She's so rude.

Mrs. Wendy walks toward the blackboard. "Let's review the contest guidelines." She points out each rule. "Open only to fifth graders. All creative work must be unpublished. Photographs must be compiled into an accepted online presentation platform. One submission per student. Ten selected finalists must recite or present their piece before a panel of judges at a special ceremony."

Several students groan about having to present in front of judges. That doesn't bother me. I mean, I'll be nervous for sure, but this contest was made for me. My family wrote the book on being first at things. Velascos are natural trailblazers. I could enter the contest and be the first student from Sendak Elementary to win it. I could finally have something to add to the trophy shelf. There's got to be a trophy, right? I raise my hand again.

"Mrs. Wendy, will the first-place winner get a trophy?" I ask.

"Let me check." She pulls a paper from the top of her desk and scans it. "First-place winner gets a trophy and two hundred dollars."

The entire classroom gasps. Now everyone's hands are up with questions. Sara and Hayley squeal back and forth at each other. "Two hundred dollars! OMG! Shopping spree!"

Mrs. Wendy shakes her head at the mayhem. "I know that's a lot of moolah, but settle down. You haven't won it yet." Mrs. Wendy underlines *APRIL 2* on the blackboard. "Now that I have your attention, keep in mind that the deadline is coming up, so if you want to enter the contest you need to get started."

A few kids groan about the deadline.

"Easy now." Mrs. Wendy tries to calm everyone down. "You've known about this contest since January. If you want to do it, there's still time, you just need to focus."

Grace turns to me, excited and red-faced. "Are you going to do it now? You totally should."

I nod. I look down at my blank Allie's List of Firsts and write: *Trailblazer Contest.* Luckily, I've got the perfect trailblazer in mind. That shiny trophy, engraved with the words *Alyssa Velasco, First-Place Winner* is going to be mine.

ChAPTER 8

In the lunch line, all my classmates are still making plans for the two-hundred-dollar prize. Diego says he's going to buy a new skateboard. Ethan says he'll donate it to the animal shelter. Grace wants to take her mom out to a nice dinner because she deserves it. Hayley and Sara want a shopping spree. I grab my tray with a plate of chicken nuggets, carrots, and Tater Tots and take my usual seat next to Grace. Sara and Hayley always sit at their own table.

I'm barely in my chair when Victor comes out of nowhere and wedges himself between Grace and me.

"What's up, Victor," I say. "Want a chicken nugget?"

"No thanks! I have my lunch." He puts a brown lunch sack on the table and pulls out an aluminum-foil-wrapped sandwich. "My mom packed me a *torta*. Want a bite?"

As he unwraps the Mexican sandwich, I gape at the *torta* filled with shredded chicken, cheese, and avocado. I'm really trying not to stare, but it is an epic *torta*. Next thing I know, all the girls are asking for a taste and Victor is more than happy to share.

"Allie, I still feel bad about ruining your volcano project, and I won't feel right until I've fixed it."

"What? There's nothing to fix. I threw it out after the science fair," I say. I dumped the big mushy pile of clay and goo into a large trash bin in the cafeteria. Good riddance!

"Not the volcano. You."

"You want to fix me?" I give him a suspicious look.

"I saw your face," Victor whispers, leaning in. "You know, today when Mrs. Wendy had the science fair winners stand up?"

I gasp because I didn't realize that he had been watching me when all of us were applauding the winners. I slide a Tater Tot across my plate, wishing I could slide right out of the cafeteria.

"You looked super depressed," Victor continues. "Like someone told you your puppy died. Like someone told you that you can't ever eat ice cream again. Like you were told to—"

"Okay, already, Victor. I wasn't depressed. I was thinking about my math homework . . . it's nothing."

Victor narrows his eyes at me like he knows it wasn't math on my mind. Maybe it's because his science project was green goo and he wears belt buckles the size of Texas with his jeans, but I doubt Victor is qualified to help me fix anything or understand how I feel. I mean, he hardly knows me.

"You really wanted to win the science fair, and I messed it up for you. Then it hit me how I can make things right. When Mrs. Wendy brought up the Trailblazer contest, everyone went nutso about the prize money, but you didn't. Instead you asked about there never being a winner from Sendak and the trophy. I know what you're after. You want a trophy. And more than that, you want to make your mark." Victor snaps his fingers.

Hearing Victor say it out loud makes my heart beat faster. I look around the table. Does everyone know how desperately I want to be first at something before I graduate from Sendak? Grace nods and gives me a sympathetic smile.

"You know about her family, right?" Grace says.

Victor shakes his head. "What about them?"

I always forget that Victor isn't from Kansas City. Of course he has no clue. My heart drops to my stomach and churns. Finally, here is someone who doesn't know my family members and can't compare me to them.

"Her big brother is Aiden," Grace offers. "Last year at Sendak, he won a full-ride scholarship to Bishop Crest Middle School. He's a soccer champ and also super cute. And then there's Ava . . ."

"She's the pretty fourth grader in all the commercials, right?" Victor says.

"That's the one." I roll my eyes. "And my big sister is Adriana," I add. "She is, like, the smartest girl in the city. She won the Mayor's Award when she was a student at Sendak. She's a legend."

"I know her." Victor shrugs. "I see Adriana every weekend."

I shake my head. There's no way he could know my sister. She's in high school.

"Whatever, Victor. How do you know her?"

"She heads the tutoring program that I go to. She comes in to work with the ESL kids every Saturday morning. I know Aiden too. When he doesn't have a soccer game, he comes to the math room where I go. Adriana is nice. She always comes in to say hi to everyone."

A wave of pride sweeps over me. Even though Adriana is super busy with school, she still finds time to volunteer with the tutoring program she founded. And it's so cool that Victor is getting tutoring. Math is really tough this year, so I can understand why he would need the extra help. He's probably not used to Sendak's high level of academics.

"Both of them are crazy smart. Adriana is going to Harvard and all that," Victor says.

My throat tightens. Just thinking about Adriana leaving makes me want to cry. "Well, she's looking at other schools too. Schools closer to home, you know," I say.

"She told me that she's going to Harvard," says Victor.

"Um, whatever. You don't know. I'm her sister," I say. "I think I would know first if she's decided on Harvard. Besides, you're missing the point. The point is that my family is super successful. My little sister, Ava, is going to win the Oscar for Best Actress someday, and Aiden will probably be the first twelve-year-old playing in the World Cup. Me? I can't even win a stupid science fair."

"*Olvídalo*. Forget about it," Victor says. "I'll help you."

"Okay, nice. I guess. But I've already decided I'm going to enter the Trailblazer contest."

"Oh." Victor drops back in his chair like he's disappointed. "I was thinking more along the lines of you being the first female Formula One or NASCAR racing champion."

"Um, you realize I am ten years old. I can't legally drive yet."

"I know, but you've got to start practicing now so that when you have your license you can start racing professionally. We should start with go-karts and work up."

"Thanks, but I'll pass."

"Okay, how about you become the first American to win the Olympic gold medal in Tae Kwon Do? You're a little *flaca*, but you could bulk up." Victor nods. "You have to join a gym, hire a coach, and practice for six hours every day. You need to start now in order to be ready for the next summer Olympics."

"I don't have six hours a day, Victor." I shake my head. "I need to win a medal now. Adriana and Aiden made Sendak history during their fifth-grade year. Ava's already made her mark. If I don't do something before the end of the school year . . ." I stop. I'm out of breath just thinking about the catastrophe it would be if I don't win something shiny and amazing before I graduate. "I have two months. That's all."

"Dang, girl" is all he can say. He takes a bite of his sandwich.

"My plan is to enter the contest with the subject being my great-gramps. He's a war hero. People can't reject a tribute to an American hero, right?" I look to Grace for confirmation.

"That would be unpatriotic," Grace says.

"The thing is . . . poetry isn't my strong point."

"Mine either," says Victor. "English is my toughest subject."

"And I'm not much of a singer-songwriter. Ava got all the talent for that. I may have to do the photo essay. Pictures are cool. I've got tons on my phone, but they're mostly of my cat, Secret."

Just then Hayley and Sara walk up to the table, across from Victor and me. "Hey, Allie," Sara says. "I need to ask you about your *bisabuelo*."

I have a bad feeling about this, but I smile anyway. "Sure, what's up?"

"I want to write a song about him for the contest. Do you think he'd be okay with that?"

My heart sinks. "What?"

"Why don't you write about your own *bisabuelo*?" Victor asks, finishing a last bite of the *torta*.

"Um, because he died when I was a baby. Thank you very much for bringing up a sad memory." Sara narrows her eyes at him in a way I've never seen her do to anyone before. She's being Hayley-fied.

"I'm sorry." Victor puts his hands up in surrender. "I didn't mean to make you upset." I feel bad for him. There's no reason for Sara to be rude, and I'm just about to say that when Hayley butts in.

"Is there a problem with her talking to your great-gramps?"

Yes. A gazillion problems. Sara should find her own inspiring family member to write a song about. Plus, I need this win more than she does. It's almost April. The clock is ticking for me to make my mark once and for all. Bisabuelo is my ticket to winning this contest. That's it. She can't write a song about my great-gramps.

I say it out loud. "Yes, there is a problem. I'm planning on doing something about him for the contest."

Sara's shoulders drop. Hayley tilts her head and crosses her arms across her chest. "Something? You don't even know what you're going to do. Plus, there's no rule saying you both can't choose the same person, so stop hating."

Hayley is such a snotty-pants. She's been that way since she started wearing pink lip gloss. Someone should really check the ingredients for that lip gloss because it's having some serious side effects.

"Fine." I shrug. "Ask him yourself, Sara, and see what he says, but you know my *bisabuelo* doesn't like it when people make a big fuss about him."

"Yes, I know. Thanks," Sara says, and leaves with Hayley.

"What's their problem?" Victor asks.

"Sara *used* to be my best friend."

"She used to be your best friend and now she wants to use your great-gramps for her contest project? Sorry, that's just coldhearted."

I shake my head. "I don't know what to do."

On her way to winning the fancy Pulitzer Prize, did Gwendolyn Brooks ever have to put up with an ex–best friend stealing her subject matter? And did she find the right words to rhyme with *betrayal*? *Traitor*? *Frenemy*?

"I know what you're going to do," says Victor. He nudges me with his elbow. "You're going to win."

Chapter 9

Once the school bell rings, all I want to do is go home and scream into my pillow, but I wait for Adriana to pick me up. Being in the same classroom all day with snooty Hayley and the traitor Sara really got me worked up. How dare she want to use my *bisabuelo* for the contest! I just know that Hayley put her up to it. Sara would never do that purposely to hurt me. Would she? She knows how important Great-Gramps is to me. She also knows how important it is to me to win a trophy for the family trophy shelf.

My head hurts like a grizzly is pressing it between its massive paws. I walk, head pounding the entire way, to the front of school, where Adriana picks Ava and me up. When I get into the car, Aiden is in the passenger seat bouncing a soccer ball on his knees, which doesn't help my headache. Ava and I take our seats in the back. She starts texting, which is fine with me because I don't want to hear about any fourth-grade drama. Today, I've got fifth-grade drama.

"We have to stop by Bisabuelo's," Adriana says. "He needs help with his computer again."

"Old people and computers should never mix," Aiden says.

Adriana and Ava giggle. I can't even muster a smirk, and Adriana notices. I just want my pillow right now.

"You okay, *hermanita*? Rough day?"

I nod.

She smiles at me through the rearview mirror.

Adriana is usually my go-to person to talk about things like this, but I haven't because I'm embarrassed about it. What kind of dork loses her best friend during the last year at elementary school? Adriana's been best friends with Michelle Logan since they were in diapers.

If I don't fix things with Sara this year, what will happen

next year at middle school? I'll have to start all over again at Bishop Crest Middle and find a new best friend.

I don't want to start over.

I gaze out the window at our neighborhood. Sara and I used to ride our bikes all the time on this street. Both of us would help Bisa in his garden and talk about going to Bishop Crest and being sixth graders. We talked about all the cool new kids we'd meet and how we could try out a new hairstyle for middle school. Now that she's hanging out with Hayley, she's already dressing differently. No comfy Keds. Now she wears ballet flats. And her hair is always worn down long like Hayley's. No more ponytails. She didn't wait for me.

My head is still pounding when we arrive at Great-Gramp's house. He lives alone in a small home that he bought before I was even born. Bisabuelo always says that when he was house-shopping he had only three rules: he didn't want any stairs to climb, he wanted a big backyard for Fourth of July barbeques, and it had to be close enough for his great-grandchildren to walk over and visit whenever we wanted. I'm there almost every day.

As soon as we arrive, Ava jumps out and snuggles up to Bisabuelo, who's sitting on the front porch swing. She leaves no room for me. Adriana and Aiden greet him with a kiss and go inside to check on his computer. I take a seat on the porch steps.

"Bisabuelo, Allie is in a grumpy mood," Ava says. "She didn't even talk to me once in the car." I glare at her. With all her texting, I'm sure she could care less.

"*¿Qué tienes*, Allie? What's wrong, *mija?*" my *bisabuelo* asks. His voice is raspy and soft today. I wonder if he's coming down with a bad cold again. A few days before Christmas, Dad had to take him to the hospital for pneumonia. We were all scared, but Great-Gramps was home with us by Christmas Eve to enjoy our traditional tamales and hot chocolate.

"Nothing," I mumble.

"See what I mean?" Ava whines. "It's so hard being Miss Grumpy's little sister."

I ignore her.

"Come here, *mija*. What's going on?"

I stand to face him. "I have a headache," I mumble.

"Do you want some aspirin, *mija*? A cup of tea?"

"No, it's just dumb school," I say, and shrug, but I feel the tears coming. I wish I could make them stop, but it's too late. Bisabuelo sees them and holds my hands.

"Tell me what's wrong, *mija*. It's okay to get it off your chest."

"Sara doesn't talk to me anymore."

"Sweet Sarita?"

"She's not so sweet," Ava quips. It's the first time I agree with Ava, but honestly I don't want to agree with her on this. I want Sara to be sweet again and to be my BFF.

"She's hardly talked to me since this semester started up, and it's getting worse. She hangs out with Hayley Ryan, who is bossy." I can't hold anything back now. It's like an emotion avalanche. "And now Sara wants to write a song about you for a contest. She just wants the prize money so she and Hayley can go on a shopping spree and buy stupid matching shirts. She could care less about anything else. So when she calls to ask if she can write a song about you, you have to tell her no. You're *my* great-gramps."

Bisabuelo studies me with his brown eyes.

"And you call me a drama queen?" Ava scoffs. She slides off the porch swing. "I'm going to see if one of my commercials comes on."

When Ava is gone, Bisabuelo speaks. "You know who you just reminded me of, Allie?"

I draw a blank and honestly I don't want to think right now. My head hurts too much.

"Who do I always say you remind me of?"

I know who he's talking about. He's told me a hundred times. "Your mom?"

"Every day, you're a little more like her, you know?"

"Was she crazy too?"

Bisabuelo chuckles. "You're not crazy, *mija*. Not only do you have her eyes and mannerisms, but you have her fighting spirit."

"I don't know what to do about Sara, Bisabuelo. I want us to be friends again, but she won't even give me a chance."

"Come sit here with me." Great-Gramps pats a space for me on the swing. I settle in next to him. "Don't you think if you talked with her you could save your friendship? You've been friends since you were babies. Just call her, invite her over, and ask her what happened. These things are done best face-to-face and not by text, or email, or whatever you kids do on those phones."

"I'm scared she won't want to talk."

"The trick is you have to be willing to listen, *mija*. You have to tell her how you feel and then listen to her. No interrupting. No thinking about what you're going to say next. Just listen. Try to understand how she feels. If she doesn't want to talk about it, then at least you've tried and you can move on and start making a new best friend."

"But I don't want a new best friend."

"More reason to talk and listen to Sara."

His words are sinking in when Adriana barges out of the house.

"Bisabuelo, I cannot believe all the emails you have from people who have seen the documentary and want to visit you. Have you responded at all? Please tell me you have."

Great-Gramps shrugs. "I meant to respond, but then I couldn't remember my password, *mija*."

"What's this about fan mail?" Ava pops her head out of the door.

"Aiden's set up a new password for you, Bisabuelo," Adriana says, ignoring Ava. "I can help you respond. Let's do it today. I insist."

"Bisa, please tell Adriana that I can help too." Ava clasps her hands like she's praying. "I'm really good at responding to fan mail. Please," Ava begs. I can't help but smile. It's fun to watch Ava squirm.

"Okay, both of you will help me. I'll be right in. Let me finish my conversation with Allie," says Bisabuelo.

"I love fan mail!" Ava jumps and squeals.

"Relax, Miss Drama. It's not your fan mail," says Adriana, and she pulls Ava inside by her stubby ponytail.

"So I can do a photo essay about you for the contest?" I ask. "The theme is a true trailblazer."

Great-Gramps rubs his chin. "A trailblazer, eh?"

"Yes, you went to war and won the Medal of Honor."

"Well, I can think of other people more worthy, but if it's what you want, *mija*," he says. I give him the tightest hug I can muster. "And if Sarita calls to ask me about the contest . . . what should I do? Do you really want me to tell your ex–best friend no?"

I swallow hard. "I guess not, but what if her project is better than mine?"

"How could it be? She won't have what I'm about to give you." Bisabuelo stands up and walks toward the door. "Come with me."

In Bisabuelo's bedroom, there are a dozen family portraits on his wall. There are photos of family I've never met because they died before I was born and yet their faces are familiar. They look like my dad, Adriana, Aiden, and Ava. I get a closer look at my grandma Esperanza and Grandpa Andres and wonder what they were like. In most of the pictures, they pose with grandchildren on their laps and look happy. Sometimes, my dad talks about them and tells funny stories until he's in tears. I guess that's how I'd feel if my parents died. I'd be sad, but I'd try to remember the funny and happy things too.

Bisabuelo pulls out a thick leather-bound scrapbook from under his bed. It's bloated and heavy with pages. He hands it to me. I'm pretty sure it weighs more than Ava and me put together. To get a better grip, I drop down on the edge of his bed.

"Here is my photo gallery." He flips through it until he's at the last few pages. "I have a few sheets left for some final memories."

I gulp hard. I don't like the way he said "final memories." I turn some pages back and see a clipped-out news article about the day my grandpa Andres was inaugurated as mayor of a small city just outside of Kansas City. I wasn't even born then. A couple pages before, there are pictures of Bisabuelo with a few of his veteran friends carrying the American flag for a parade. I flip a few more pages, and there are black-and-white photos of my *bisabuelo* in Italy, where he served in the war.

"These are great, Bisa," I say. "These are really going to help me win."

There are pictures of him digging foxholes and pictures of him posing with other soldiers. Bisa was so young. There are even a few of him with some pretty Italian women, but the one that catches my eye is the photo of him with President Truman receiving his Congressional Medal of Honor. These are the photos I need for the contest. When people see these pictures of my war hero Bisabuelo, they will be begging me to take first prize.

I move on to photographs of Ava in the school musical this past fall. She was the first fourth grader to land the lead role in a Sendak school musical. Usually it goes to a fifth grader, but Ava won the role fair and square. At first, some fifth graders and parents complained, but her performance silenced them. Our principal, Mr. Vihn, said that "Ava Velasco sings and dances like she was born on Broadway." As much as she can be a brat, I'm really proud of Ava.

I turn another page, and there's me posing with my volcano a few days before the science fair. That first-place trophy should have been mine. I should be home polishing it right now.

"You should take this photo out. I didn't win the science fair," I mumble. "No trophy. No first place. *Nada*. It makes me sad."

"Let me show you something." Bisabuelo flips the pages to a tattered black-and-white photo of a young woman with a baby on her lap and a boy about Aiden's age standing next to her. It takes a while, but I recognize that the boy is

Bisabuelo. "This is my mother, Adela Salazar, the day of my father's funeral."

For as long as I remember, my *bisabuelo* has always told me that I remind him of her, but I have never seen this picture of her until now. In it, she has on a black dress. I search her delicate, heart-shaped face and see the resemblance. It is like an older version of me. Her midnight-dark hair is pulled back, which gives extra focus on her wide, serious gaze.

"She never won a trophy in her life, but she made a difference in this world. You know, I almost didn't get to go to school when I was your age."

"Why not?"

"It was a different time back then, *mija*. I was poor and didn't speak any English, but my mom had dreams for my brother and me. She tried to enroll me at school, but every school turned us away. Finally, we got to this one school almost a whole town away from where we lived. And again, we were refused at the front door. The school headmaster didn't even let us enter the school. Can you imagine that? They wouldn't even let us inside.

"The principal pretended that she didn't understand my mom's poor English and told her to try another school, but we had already tried everywhere else. This school was our last chance. I had never seen my mom so dejected. I thought she was going to give up. So I turned to leave. But my mom stopped me. She grabbed my baby brother from me, faced the lady again, and said a few more things. This time the woman understood my mother's English. The next thing I knew, the lady enrolled me right there on the spot. I started school that day."

"What did your mom say to her?"

"She offered to mend all the woman's clothes and make her some new dresses. That's what did it. So every day, after my mom left her sewing job, she worked on new dresses for the principal while I learned English. That's how I got my education, but there were no photography contests for me. And I think I could have been a great photographer like Robert Capa."

"Who?"

"One of the best photojournalists in history, *mija*."

"Did he win any awards?"

"Awards or not, the point is he was a great photographer, Allie."

I gaze over the photo some more. I wonder if Robert Capa took pictures like this one. Maybe taking a picture of a poor Mexican family wouldn't have interested him, but I can't take my eye off the photo. Bisabuelo says that I'm like his mom, but would I be brave enough to stand up to a school principal? Would I ever be clever enough to find a way for a child to go to school? That sounds more like Adriana.

All I know is that I want to win like Gwendolyn with the Pulitzer or Junko taking her pickax to the top of a mountain. And like my great-gramps's mom, Adela Salazar, I have to be brave. I will do whatever it takes to win this contest and live up to my family's accomplishments.

Chapter 10

I close the scrapbook. "Thank you, Bisabuelo. This is seriously going to help me win."

"It's yours to use." He pats me on the arm before turning to leave the room. "Now, I have to do some work. Your sister insists that I write emails."

"What do those people write you about?"

He pauses at the doorway. "They mostly want to thank me for being a good soldier. Sometimes they invite me to their homes for dinner because they want to talk about the war."

"You don't mind that?"

"It's tough sometimes for me to talk about it. There are things I don't want to dredge up, but it's important for people to connect and talk things over."

"That's why you like to go to the veterans' center? You like to talk to the other soldiers?"

"*Sí, mija.* These young vets have been through a lot. I like to listen to them, let them know there is life after war. They're not alone."

He leaves the room, and I pick up the phone next to his bed. I should call Sara like he said . . . but I'm not ready. Instead, I take the scrapbook with me to the living room where Ava is lounging in my *bisabuelo*'s La-Z-Boy chair, watching TV.

This scrapbook is everything I need for the contest. How can I not win with all these cool black-and-white photos of my *bisa* in Italy?

"Allie! You missed my commercial. It came on after the talk show ended. Maybe it'll air again."

"Oh, I really hope so," I say with just an ounce of sarcasm.

"Grumpy-butt."

I make myself comfortable on the couch and spread the scrapbook across my lap. Ava joins me. "What are you doing?"

"Going through Bisa's scrapbook."

"For your contest?" she asks.

"Don't worry about it," I say. "Just watch TV. I bet one of your commercials is about to come on."

She turns away, suspiciously silent. Even though I'm trying to ignore her, I can see she's thinking really hard by the way she squints her eyes and bites her lower lip. Suddenly, she turns back to me with a big smile. "Guess who wrote a poem for you?" she says. "I did! It's about you. Want to hear it?"

"Go for it."

"There was a girl named Allie
Who complained that she lost her friend,
So she became grumpy,
Her day was all dumpy,
And she wished she'd never left her bed."

I shake my head, stunned. How did she make that up so fast?

"You're welcome." She giggles, and faces the TV again just in time to catch a Sifuentes Auto Mart commercial.

The phone rings. I pick it up.

"Hello, may I speak to Mr. Rocky Velasco, please?" I recognize the voice right away.

"Sara?"

"Oh, hey, Allie. You're at your great-gramp's house, huh?"

"Yep, he's helping me with my project." I take the phone with its long extension into the other room for some privacy. This is my chance to talk to Sara.

"Oh, that's why I was calling. I want to ask your great-gramps if I could interview him for my song. Is he there?"

"Yes, he's here, but he's really busy right now. Can you wait a few minutes? I wanted to ask you something anyway."

"Um, okay," Sara says, sounding unsure.

I take a deep breath and try to remember what my great-gramps said about listening. More listening. Less talking. Isn't that what he said?

"Sara, why don't you talk to me anymore?"

"I talk to you . . . I just spoke to you today," she says.

"Hardly," I answer back, with more snap than I intended. "Is it because of Hayley? I know she's the one that put you up to writing a song about my *bisabuelo* for the contest. You only spoke to me to ask about my *bisabuelo* because Hayley wants you to steal my idea." My heart is pumping fast.

"Hayley didn't know you wanted to enter a project about your *bisabuelo*. I didn't know either. We were talking about the contest at lunch, and I thought your *bisabuelo* would be the perfect subject because he's a war hero."

"But you and I used to sit together at lunch and talk. Now it's you and Hayley all the time." I don't mean to whine, but it pours out of me. I'm ready to complain some more about how she never invites me to her house anymore and even though I've invited her several times she always says she's busy with something, but before I start up again, I rewind what she just said.

"Wait a minute . . ." I say. "Did you say it was your idea? Wasn't it Hayley's?"

"It was my idea, Allie. I think I could win writing a song about him. I mean, like I said, he's a famous war hero."

"But he's my trailblazer."

"So what?" she says. I can feel her shrug though the phone, and it burns me. "Like Hayley said, there's no rule about submitting a project on the same person."

"You only want to use him to win the two hundred dollars," I snap. "I heard you and Hayley talking about a shopping spree."

"And you are just after the first-place trophy. That's all you ever care about. First place this. First place that. Like with the Furry Friends Photo Contest. I thought it was something fun we could do together over holiday break to help the animal shelter, but you shot down every single one of my ideas for the photo with Secret. You're like a crazed

83

Chihuahua whenever you're trying to win something. It's super annoying. Like now with this contest."

"Hey! That's not true!" I exclaim. My stomach tightens into a big knot. Is that really the reason? Has it been about Secret and the Furry Friends Photo Contest this whole time? Did I really shoot down all her ideas? I don't think so. She's just trying to hurt my feelings. I'm not a crazed Chihuahua!

Great-Gramps told me to listen to her and I'm really trying, but now she's just being rude. "Whatever, Sara," I say.

"Whatever," she says. "So can I talk to your great-gramps now?"

"Sorry, he left." I hang up the phone, and my head throbs. Talking to her was one big fail.

I hate to admit it, but Ava's poem was right. My day has been dumpy, and I wish I'd just stayed in bed this morning.

Chapter 11

The next day at school, I avoid Sara. When I told Adriana last night that I hung up on Sara, she gave me the world's longest disappointed stare. It lasted like five minutes and twenty-nine seconds. Finally, she said that I have to apologize, but I don't see any reason for it. If anything, Sara should apologize to me. She's the one who called me a crazed Chihuahua and is writing a song about my *bisabuelo* just to spite me. She wants to win the prize money. She could care less about my great-gramps.

"Well, isn't that why you chose him too . . . for the tro-phy?" Victor says after I complain to him. Victor and I are in second-hour math class. We're supposed to be working on a group assignment with Diego and Grace, but really they are doing all the problems and Victor and I are talking. "You want to win a trophy and make your mark before you gradu-ate, right? *Es lo mismo.*"

"It's not the same," I growl. "I'm doing it to make a trib-ute to my *bisa*. He's a true trailblazer. Sara, on the other hand, is doing it so she and Hayley can go buy matching leggings. It's totally different."

Diego looks up at us in exasperation. "C'mon, you guys, we have to finish these problems before the end of class," he says. "Forget Sara. If you guys can take problems ten through twenty, we'll be done."

Victor nods and gets to work, scribbling computations in the workbook.

I narrow in on the math problems in front of me. Ques-tions number ten to twenty are missing mean, range, and median problems. It's simple stuff that I can usually knock out in a few minutes, but I can't stop thinking about Sara and what hanging the phone up on her means. Is it the end of our friendship for good?

I look over at Sara and Hayley huddled over the math handouts. Sara and I had been best friends since we were four years old. Is our friendship range only six years? I stare at the math problems. I can't make any sense of them.

"Done!" Victor announces. He puts his pencil down. My worksheet is blank. Defeated again.

"With all ten problems?" Diego asks, and leans in to look at Victor's worksheet.

"How did you get done so fast?" Grace asks.

I put my pencil down with a thud on my desk. I should be the first one done. Instead I'll be the last, and it's because I've been worrying over stupid Sara. Mrs. Wendy rings her little bell and tells us to wrap it up and turn in our worksheets.

"Here, Allie, take mine." Victor offers his worksheet.

"No, it's okay. I'll stay after if I have to. I'll get it done."

"Take it, Allie. It was a group assignment anyway," Grace adds. "We're supposed to share."

"It just so happens that some of us shared more than others," Diego says. "Just sayin'."

"Thanks." I take Victor's worksheet and quickly start copying down the answers. As I copy, I review all the answers. Everything looks good.

"Wow, Victor. The tutoring program must really be helping you."

"What do you mean?"

"You said you attend the tutoring program on Saturdays. I can definitely see it's working. Good job."

Victor leans back in his chair, narrows his eyes, and gives me this quiet closed-mouth smile like he's keeping a secret.

I put my name on the top of my worksheet, but I feel bad because none of it is my work. As I turn it in to Mrs. Wendy, I promise myself I'll make it up somehow. Before leaving the classroom, I pause at the poster of Gwendolyn Brooks. I bet the whole time she was writing her book of poetry that won the Pulitzer Prize, Gwendolyn didn't waste one single second worrying about any backstabbing friends. If I'm ever going to win first place, I have to stop freaking out about Sara.

CHAPTER 12

Gwendolyn Brooks was thirteen years old when she published her first poem. That's three years older than me. Twenty years later, she won the big enchilada: the Pulitzer. She spent twenty years writing poems before winning that big award. I haven't been doing anything for five or even two years. The only poems I've written have been for school assignments. In fourth grade, I wrote a rhyming poem about how my life was like strawberry ice cream. Cool and sweet. Rosy like my dreams. Life is a frozen treat. Strawberry ice cream.

I got an A for it.

This last year at Sendak has not even been close to sweet like strawberry ice cream. Instead, it's been like a scoop of ice cream dropped splat on the sidewalk.

Anyway, I have a feeling that a rhyming poem comparing my *bisabuelo* to ice cream isn't going to cut it for this contest. Nor will a bunch of selfies I've taken with my phone. I need real war photos. Black-and-white war photos. Luckily, I have my *bisa*'s photo album. Now I just need to find some facts about the war and tell my Bisa's trailblazing story as a super-awesome war hero.

In the library, I've gathered a tower of books for my project. There are so many books that I'm starting to feel like they will tumble and cover me in an information avalanche. Where do I even start?

On the wall across from me there's a poster of an Olympic runner crossing the finish line. It says *Billy Mills, First American to win the 10,000 meter gold medal.*

"Need some help?" Victor plops down across from me at the table. His eyes follow my gaze to the poster.

"Yes, help me to understand why everywhere I go there are people like this Billy Mills guy winning medals, being the first at something amazing, being turned into posters and taped up onto walls just to taunt me."

"I think it's cool. I remember seeing a video about this guy," Victor says. "No one thought he'd win. He came all the way from the middle of the pack to win the race in the last seconds. Super fast." Victor smiles at the picture like it's him crossing the finish line. "Hey, if you want to win a race, I could help you. I mean, we'd have to train every day. We should start with an easy 5K run—"

"No, it's not that. I just need all the help I can get to beat Sara and win this contest."

Victor eyes the tower of books. "Are you planning to read all these books?"

"Not really, I just need some facts."

"Let me make this simpler for you," Victor says, and then he stands up and picks up the tower of books, leaving only two on the table.

"What are you doing?" I ask in the quietest scream I can manage because we are in the library. The last thing I need is to have Mrs. Chambers, the librarian, kick me out. Victor takes the books to the restock shelf. Mrs. Chambers is going to love that! We'll both be kicked out for sure.

When he comes back, I'm red-hot. "Why are you always sabotaging me?"

"I'm helping you. You have two very good books right there. That's enough. The only other thing you need to do is to talk to your *bisabuelo*, take some photos, create a story-board telling his story, organize it on Prezi, and submit it."

I look down at the books. He's right. "A storyboard." I write that down in my notebook. "That's genius. Thanks." I just have to win this contest. "My *bisabuelo* loaned me his photo album. It's full of really cool pictures from his time in the war."

"Can I see it sometime? That sounds awesome."

I nod. "Sure, I'll let you see it when I'm done. Anyway, if I can't win with his photos and his story, then I'm never going to win and I'll have to accept that I'm not a true Velasco. Do you think I could be adopted?"

Victor shakes his head and snorts. "Okay, you're going overboard now."

We sit there silent for a few seconds.

"Thank you for wanting to help me," I finally say. I open one of the books left on the table. It's full of photographs of destroyed European cities and D-day photos. "Can I ask you something?"

"Sure." He also opens a book.

"Are you helping me because you still feel guilty about ruining my volcano project? Because if so—"

Victor winces. "I still feel really bad about that."

"You don't have to feel guilty. I forgave you already."

He nods at me. "It's that and something else." He looks down at the book. "I'm going to be the first in my family to graduate from high school someday. So I know how you feel wanting to do your best for your family."

"The first to graduate from high school?" I regret how surprised I sound, but it's out there and I can't shove it back into my mouth now. "Sorry, I just mean—"

"I know. Everyone at Sendak has parents that are super educated and rich. My parents never went higher than sixth grade. I'm like Billy Mills. I'm starting out the underdog, but I'm going to catch up. I have to."

"But why only sixth grade?"

"They were poor in Mexico. My dad had to work to help his family and couldn't finish school. My mom lived in a small village where the nearest school was in a whole other city. Even though she wanted to go, her family didn't have money to send her and her brothers. You've been to Mexico, right? You know how it is for the poor families there."

"Yes, I know." And I really do. Two years ago, my family and I traveled with my *bisabuelo* to the town in Mexico where his mother was born. Now that I think of it, that's one of the last trips my *bisabuelo* went on before the doctor told him traveling was too much of a health risk. While there, we mostly stayed near a beach resort area with fancy shops, but when searching for his mom's community, we visited areas where there were no paved roads and homes made of cement blocks, plastic bags, and ragged pieces of wood and tin. Children in ripped clothes sold gum and plastic flowers in the streets.

I lower my head because Victor's story is sad. I feel bad for anyone who can't get everything they need. I complain a lot about school, but at least I get to go to school and don't have to spend all day selling gum in the streets just to eat. And my school is air-conditioned on hot days, and has bathrooms with running water, a cafeteria that serves pizza, a big soccer field, and a library filled with books and computers.

"It's up to me to be the first and show my little brother and sisters that they can do it too," Victor says. "I've applied for Bishop Crest Middle."

"That's where I'm going!" I say excitedly. "That's where all of my family goes." It's also where all the Sendak students go as long as they don't royally mess up at Sendak and their families can afford it, which most of them can. "I hope you don't take this the wrong way, but how will you afford it? Do you have a secret stash of gold somewhere?" I joke.

"That's why I need a scholarship big-time. If I don't, I'll have to go to another school and we won't see each other."

"I'm sure you'll get a scholarship." I smile. I don't want to be the one to crush his dream. "But we'll be friends no matter where you go," I say. I really mean that.

"Thanks, Allie. The thing is, I'm not going to stop at high school. I plan to go to this big college called MIT to study engineering. How about you? Do you think you'll go to Harvard like Adriana?"

"Well . . ." I frown. He still thinks Adriana is going to leave me and our family for a stupid ivy school in Massachusetts. "First things first, I have to win this contest. I have to make my mark at Sendak."

"You've got this, Allie," Victor says. "Just don't ever give up."

"I won't give up if you don't give up," I say back to him.

"You've got a deal." Victor holds out his hand to seal it with a handshake. I shake his hand but can't help giggling.

I turn a few more pages of the war book in front of me. Victor turns some pages too. I smile at him when he's not looking. Did Billy Mills have someone in his life like Victor? A friend that helped him cross the finish line? I bet he did. Somehow when I'm around Victor, I feel ready to win a hundred prizes.

ChapteR 13

The first thing I do when I get to Bisabuelo's house is give him a big smooch on his cheek and grab his scrapbook. Next week is the deadline, and I don't want to waste a moment.

At the dinner table, I draw up a storyboard and start pulling photos from his photo album. My favorite photos are of him as a young soldier. I find one of him with another soldier standing in a foxhole with shovels in their hands.

"How deep were the foxholes, Bisa?"

He comes over and sits with me at the table. He takes the photo from my hand and gazes long at it. "They had to be deep enough for a soldier to sleep, sit, and stand in. So about six feet deep," Bisa says. He hands the photo back to me. "Whenever we weren't in combat, it seemed like we were digging these holes. We slept, ate, and played cards in them."

The foxholes look big enough for a coffin to fit, but I don't say this to him. "Was it hard, Bisa? To sleep in them?"

He nods. "Over time you learn to live with the dirt, the rain, the mud. All of that is better than bullets," he says, and gives me a wink. I don't know what to say to that. I'm just grateful that a bullet never got him. "I think I have what I need, Bisa. I've picked out my favorite photos. There's just one more I need. I would like a photo of you with your Medal of Honor award. I think that will be the game changer. A photo of you, as you are now, holding the medal."

"You think so, eh?"

"It will show all that you've achieved in life—"

The doorbell rings. Bisa leaves the table to answer it. In walk Sara and Hayley. I feel every muscle in my neck tense up, so I hover over the scrapbook trying to look super focused. When Sara passes me to head into the kitchen for a glass of lemonade, she gives me a cold "Hi, Allie." I don't say anything back, and Bisabuelo notices. He pats my shoulder. Out of respect to him, I mind my manners and greet them both with a curt "Hey."

I suppose I should be happy Sara said anything to me at all, especially since I hung up on her, but her presence at my *bisa*'s home is like an enemy invasion. I wish I had a foxhole to hide in right now. When they have their glasses full of lemonade, they head back to the living room. From the corner of my eye, I see Sara take a seat on the couch and pull out her pen and notebook.

"Allie, *mija*. Why don't you come join us?" Bisabuelo yells to me. "You girls don't mind, do you?"

After a few seconds, Sara finally speaks up. "I don't mind, Bisabuelo."

"No, I don't mind, Mr. Velasco," Hayley says.

"*Qué bueno.*"

I grab my glass of lemonade and take a seat on the chair next to him.

"Bisabuelo, thank you for letting us come over. I'm writing a song about you for the Trailblazer contest. I'm sure Allie told you about it?"

Bisabuelo nods.

"I'd like to make it a Mexican *corrido*, in tribute to you."

I roll my eyes. She should be writing a song about someone in her own family and leave mine alone!

"*Mija*, I'm happy to help. And you know I love a good *corrido*," Bisa says. "We go back a long way . . . Allie, how long have you and Sarita been friends?"

I stare at the ice cubes in my lemonade. "Since we were four, I guess. I don't remember."

"So many years!" Bisabuelo smiles.

"That's right." Sara nods.

"That's very special when you have friends like that." Bisabuelo looks back and forth at both of us. "All my childhood friends are dead. Somehow, I've outlived them all. Can you believe that, girls? In the shape I'm in?" He taps his cane that's leaned up against the La-Z-Boy.

Sara and Hayley giggle. I count the cushions on Bisa's couch.

"So I need to know your story. Can you tell me about the war?" Sara asks in a gentle voice that reminds me of the old Sara. She used to have a kind voice. Now at school she talks like Hayley. It's high-pitched and annoying like an alarm clock, but there's no snooze button on either of them. I wish there was, I'd push it right now. "I know it can be hard for you to talk about the war, but I remember from the documentary that—"

"You've seen the documentary?" Bisabuelo asks, surprised.

"Our class went on a field trip to see it," Sara answers.

"I'm so sorry. How boring for you."

"No, I liked it. All of us liked it," Sara says, and looks at me and Hayley.

"It was better than having to read a book about the war," Hayley says, and my *bisabuelo* thinks that's so funny that he laughs and smacks his thigh.

"Well, that and the fact that it was a documentary about someone we know," Sara adds, and then she looks at me with a slight smile. "After we watched it, everyone begged Allie to get your autograph. Remember, Allie?"

I nod but don't smile back. "Yeah."

"We were going to charge the other kids for it, but at the last minute, we chickened out," Sara confesses. I gasp. I can't believe she's telling him this. Even though we didn't go through with it, I've never told Bisa about our autograph plot because I know he wouldn't approve. We were going to charge everyone at school a dollar each for the autographed postcards so that we could throw an end-of-year dance party with a DJ and everything.

"Was that why I was signing all those postcards for you girls?"

I try not to giggle, but I can't help it when Sara starts laughing.

"Don't worry, we didn't charge anyone. I promise," I say.

"Ah, you never collected, eh? Your conscience got to you . . . that's good."

Sara then looks up at me like she just remembered something. "It was fun."

Hayley writhes around like she's sitting on a pile of her own lip gloss or like she's just seen the ghost of friendship past. She and Sara don't have memories like Sara and I do. Take that, Hayley!

"In the documentary, it said you joined when you were only seventeen years old. You lied to the army recruiter to get in. Why was it so important for you to go to war?"

Bisabuelo leans forward. "I signed up for two reasons. Hitler was an evil man that needed a good hard smack, and I thought I could help the United States deliver that smackdown."

Now we all laugh.

"And second, I wanted a better life for my mom, my little brother, and any future family I might have. I knew there was a good chance I'd die, but it seemed worth it. I had to try to get that American dream everyone talked about, and I knew I'd have to go to war to get a piece of it."

"Do you feel like you've achieved it?" Sara asks. "The American dream?"

My heart thumps hard in my chest. Before he even knew me, Bisabuelo was thinking of me. Thinking of his future family and willing to sacrifice his life for us. I sit at the edge of the chair waiting for his response.

"Yes, *mija*. I do," he says, lost in some deep memory. "It came at a cost. A high cost, but I believe I have achieved the American dream."

I know that when he says "high cost," he means his little brother who died from illness while he was in the war and then mother, the mother I remind him of, that he lost shortly after he returned. For so many years after the war, my *bisabuelo* was alone without any family to help him. I want to cry, but I don't dare. Not in front of Sara and Hayley. I take a sip of lemonade and think about something happy like baby sloths, chocolate ice cream . . .

"Did you see anyone die?" Hayley asks.

"Hayley!" I snap. I watch Bisabuelo's face tighten like when he has a coughing fit. Haley just gets on my nerves.

"You don't have to answer if it's too difficult, Bisa," Sara says.

"It's a good question," Bisabuelo says. "It's an honest question. And I'm going to give you an honest answer that I hope you can understand even though you're so young," he says with a tender smile.

Sara sits up straight and readies her pen and notebook.

"Young men died all around me the whole time I was in the European Theater. In the movies they glorify war, but it's ugly business. I was only a few days into it when a buddy of mine died in front of me. I can barely remember my phone number and address these days," Bisa says. "But I still remember his face and name."

"What did you do?" Sara asks.

"For a moment, I lost it. I stopped doing my job. So my sergeant pulled me up by my collar and yelled at me, 'Men don't cry.' He shoved the radio back into my hands and told me to get up and move." Bisabuelo leans back into his La-Z-Boy. "I realized later that my sergeant was teaching me to survive." He pauses and closes his eyes. I wonder if he's back in Italy. "And the truth is men do cry and there's nothing wrong with that." Bisabuelo reopens his eyes. They are wet and I know he can't continue.

"Are you okay, Bisabuelo?" I ask. "I think that's enough, Sara," I say, and Sara nods.

"Couldn't you just answer a few more quest—" Hayley presses.

"Hayley, that's it," Sara says and closes her notebook. "It's enough. I've got enough."

Sara's tone of voice startles me. Hayley pouts. I want to throw a couch pillow at Hayley, but Sara's apologetic expression stops me.

"Sorry," she says. "We didn't mean to make you sad, Bisa."

Bisabuelo grabs our hands. "No, I'm sorry, *mija*. It's just tough. You both would have a better chance of winning if you picked a better subject and not a *viejo* like me. Who wants to hear a song about an old man?"

"I do." I nod.

"Thank you so much. I promise that I'll write a decent *corrido* for you," Sara says, and stands to leave. Hayley follows her. "I'll try my best."

"I know you'll do a great job, *mija*." Bisabuelo gets up slowly and hugs both of them good-bye.

Sara turns to me. "See you at school, Allie. Don't forget Monday is April Fool's Day," she says as she slips out the door with Hayley.

"Oh, that's right," I answer back. I'm grateful for the reminder because April Fool's Day is a big deal at Sendak.

I don't close the front door behind them right away. Instead, I watch as Sara exchanges a few words with Hayley. I can't hear what she's saying, but from the looks of it, Sara is not happy. It's the closest sign I've seen in days that there may still be a chance for Sara and me to be best friends again.

ChapTeR 14

Monday may be April Fool's Day, but today, Saturday, March 30, is Adriana's seventeenth birthday. And since it's the day she tutors ESL at the community center, my family is taking a huge ice cream cake and a star piñata to the center. Adriana loves celebrating her birthday with all the kids. Last year, some of the older tutors performed a choreographed dance number to her favorite song. At the end, they made all of us get up and dance too. We had a blast. After that, the little kids serenaded her with the Spanish birthday song "*Las mañanitas.*" It was super cute.

When we get to the center, it's already decorated with red balloons and there's a big banner that reads *Happy Birthday, Adriana!* hung from the ceiling. Mostly, the center is quiet because tutoring is in session. Everyone is either in the English or math room. Only the program manager, Mr. Cushinberry, is there to greet us and show us where to set up the cake. While Aiden and Ava get to work taking red paper plates, napkins, and forks out of the grocery sack, I help Mom prepare the fruit punch because she says she wants to talk to me.

"How's your Trailblazer contest submission going?" she asks me. "Do you have everything you need?"

"I think so. I worked on it last night. I still have more to do."

"Good girl. The reason I ask is because I have something for you." She stops pouring ginger ale into the punch bowl and pulls a camera from her leather bag. "It's an old camera from work. I thought you could put it to use for your contest."

"What's that antique?" Aiden slaps his hands together and points at the camera. "Ha! Now Allie has to lug a clunky camera around all day."

"Hey, mister! It's a state-of-the-art digital camera," my mom says. "You just worry about those napkins." She turns back to me. "I thought it might help. Those cell phone pictures of yours won't cut it in a contest like this. I want you to have a fighting chance." She kisses me on the forehead. "Remember, the best photographers can tell a whole story with one single image."

"Listen to your mom—she's an award-winning news anchor and will once again be crowned best news anchor tonight," Dad says, and kisses my mom's cheek before jetting off to hang the piñata with Mr. Cushinberry.

I drape the camera around my neck. It's heavy, but I'd lug a boulder the size of Mexico around my neck if it'd help me win.

"Are you going to win again, Mom?" I ask.

She wipes her hands on her apron. "Oh, I don't know. I've won three years in a row. Maybe it's time someone else won for a change, you know?"

"Would you be upset if you didn't win?"

"I'm not going to lie, it feels better to win, Alyssa." She grins slyly. "The recognition is nice. It's validation for the work I'm doing."

"And you get a trophy, right?"

"Yes, Alyssa. There's a trophy involved, but it's the recognition I value most."

I hold the camera up and look through the lens. Maybe this camera is exactly what I need to take a photograph of Great-Gramps with his Medal of Honor. I take a photo of my mom, and she laughs. She poses with the punch bowl like one of those ladies on a TV cooking show. "My mom, the award-winning news anchor and punch maker," I say.

"Mom, it's so not fair! Aiden has a birthday card for Adriana, and I don't!" Ava groans. "I just put cash in an envelope." Ava pulls out a white envelope from her purse. "Do you think that's okay?"

"How much are you giving her?" Aiden grabs the white envelope from her hand.

"It's not for her. It's for the scholarship," Mom says as he opens the envelope.

"There's fifty dollars in here!" Aiden exclaims. "You're banking it from all those commercial gigs you're getting, huh?"

"That's right, I win again!" says Ava.

"Aiden and Ava, it's not about the amount. It's about the cause you're helping," Mom says, and shakes her head.

I walk over to see the crisp fifty-dollar bill. Ulysses S. Grant stares back at me. I can't believe it. My little sister has serious moolah. Adriana makes it clear to everyone that she doesn't accept birthday gifts. Since she started the program, she's asked family and friends to instead make donations to the It Takes a Village scholarship so that two deserving tutors can receive a scholarship for school.

"I'd have more, but Mom and Dad make me save it in my bank account," Ava pouts. "Mom says it's for my future." Ava grabs the envelope from Aiden and puts it back into her bag. "My future is in Hollywood."

Aiden snorts. Mom rolls her eyes.

"Yes, Ava. But it's still good to have a backup plan and to save for a rainy day," Mom says.

"Backup plans are for losers," Aiden says. "That's what my coach told us."

Mom lets out a long sigh.

I stack the cups next to the punch bowl. Mom kisses my head and moves on to help my dad with the piñata. Tucked inside the homemade birthday card I've made for Adriana is twenty-five dollars. I know it isn't much. It certainly isn't fifty dollars. Unlike Ava, I've earned all the scholarship money from doing extra chores around the house. Plus, Bisa gave me five dollars for going to the store for him, although I told him he didn't need to pay me. I only accepted it because I told him it'd go toward the scholarship. Speaking of scholarships . . .

"Aiden, do you know a kid named Victor Garcia that comes here for help with math? He's from Texas," I ask.

"He's the kid always wearing those big belt buckles, right?"

I nod. That's Victor Garcia for sure.

"He comes here, but not for help. He's a math tutor."

I stop messing with the napkins. "What?"

"Yeah, he's almost as good as me when it comes to math. Almost. Can't say the same for his soccer game, though." Aiden chuckles.

"Are you sure he's a tutor?"

"Um, yeah. I know because I'm a tutor. Duh."

I'm confused. This whole time I thought Victor was being tutored because math class is so tough this year.

I leave the napkins in a neat stack and walk to the math room to see for myself. Once inside, I spot Victor right away at a table with four other kids. He's wearing a red It Takes a Village T-shirt, which is what all the tutors wear. As I approach, Victor sees me and shouts, "Hey, volcano girl!" He gets up and meets me halfway. "Here for Adriana's birthday party?"

I nod. "Why didn't you tell me you tutored?" I ask.

Victor chuckles and looks down at his feet and then back at me with his warm brown eyes. "I told you that I knew

Adriana because of the tutoring program. You just assumed that I was being tutored."

I feel my face turn red, and so I look down at my dumb flip-flops. He's right. I did assume that he was being tutored. I don't know why I did that. Victor gives me a gentle nudge.

"It's okay, Allie. I'm used to people underestimating me. You're not the first."

"That's a first I don't want." And I really mean that. I feel like a big dork.

"When my parents enrolled me at Sendak, my score on the entry exam was so high, they thought I cheated. They didn't say that, but I think they took one look at my family and me and assumed that—"

"You weren't smart enough."

"Exacto."

"That's unfair," I say, and think back to the story my *bisabuelo* told me about how he was refused at the door of a school because they also prejudged his mom and my great-gramps.

Victor shrugs. "Anyway, I had to take the test again, and this time in the vice principal's office. He watched me until I finished. Talk about uncomfortable, but I passed again."

"Way to go, Victor."

He nods and smiles. Around the room, there are posters

of famous scientists, astronauts, and technology pioneers like Steve Jobs and Bill Gates. However, I move toward the poster of Sonia Sotomayor, the first Hispanic Supreme Court justice.

The day she was sworn into the Supreme Court, Adriana celebrated like it was New Year's Eve. "Do you know what this means, Allie?" she had asked. "For nearly forever, the Supreme Court has been all male, and now there are two women on it and one is a Latina like us."

Since then, Elena Kagan had joined the Supreme Court, bringing the number of women up to three. I focus on Sotomayor's smiling face. "I wonder if when Judge Sotomayor was a little girl she ever thought she'd be the first Hispanic Supreme Court justice someday. Did she dream about it? Was she first at other things too?"

"She was the first in her family to go to an Ivy League school. I read that. Just like Adriana will be," Victor says.

"Did Judge Sotomayor have a little sister that didn't want her to go so far away?" I ask.

"I don't know." He shrugs. "Why are you so against Adriana going to Harvard? Not everyone gets into Harvard, you know? You of all people should be happy about that," Victor says. He's right. I should be happy, but I will miss Adriana too much.

"I just don't want her to be so far from me. She's the only one that helps me."

"The only one?" Victor crosses his arms and narrows his eyes at me. "How about your great-gramps? What about me?"

The way Victor looks at me makes my whole face warm up. He's right again. He's been a good friend.

"Have you heard anything from Bishop Crest about being accepted or getting a scholarship yet?"

Victor shakes his head. "Not yet. The wait is driving me crazy."

I remember waiting for my acceptance letter. For me, there was never a doubt I'd get in. I've attended the right school since kindergarten, and my dad and Adriana both graduated from Bishop Crest Middle. Aiden is a star athlete and student there now. There was no question I'd be accepted, but I still remember the painful wait for the official letter. The longer the letter took to arrive, the more nails I chewed away. Sara and I texted each other every day about whether or not our letters had shown up. When that glorious cream-colored enveloped with the Bishop Crest logo arrived over the summer, Sara and I celebrated with homemade smoothies.

"Don't worry, Victor. When that letter arrives, we'll celebrate," I say.

The door opens, and Victor's four younger siblings run into the room and latch on to him. They are as cute and tiny as I remember from when we met at the science fair.

"How'd you do in class today?" Victor asks, and ruffles his little brother's hair. Each of them shows off the gold star stickers they received. "I'm so proud of you." Victor gives each of them a kiss on their heads, and they light up like candles on a birthday cake. "Are you ready to sing *'Las mañanitas'* to Adriana?" All four nod excitedly and giggle. *"Qué bien."*

"Let me get a quick photo of you guys." As I take a few more photos of their beaming faces, chills run through me. Victor's tenderness toward his younger siblings reminds me of my *bisabuelo.*

"Nice!" I say.

I'd miss Victor if he weren't at Bishop Crest with me next year. I bite down on my bottom lip with worry. I have to ask Adriana for a favor. There's a way she could help Victor. But first, I have to know once and for all if she is really leaving for Harvard. I wish she'd never applied. If she is truly heading to Harvard, leaving me, then why am I the last to know?

Chapter 15

After the piñata, the serenades, dancing, and cake, we return home, pooped. Victor taught me how to dance Texas cumbia, and we danced for an hour straight. It was super fun. I took tons of photos with my new camera of Adriana and Bisabuelo dancing too.

Adriana has already showered, changed, and left with her girlfriends for a birthday pizza and movie night. From my bedroom window, I watched her jump into Michelle's Jeep. I can't wait till I'm old enough to go off with my girl-friends for a pizza and movie night. It'd be so cool to be out and not have parents around nagging at you to finish the crust. The way things are going with Sara, I'll be lucky if I have any *amigas* to take me out for my birthday. At least there's Victor. Maybe someday Victor and I will be running off to go see a movie and have pizza together on my birthday. That'd be cool.

Mom and Dad quickly changed into fancy clothes for the award ceremony. I'm sure tomorrow there will be a new shiny trophy next to her other awards on the shelf. Before leaving, Mom announced, "Aiden's in charge," which is fine with me because that means he'll play video games all night and leave me alone. I have serious work to do on my presentation.

I've completed my storyboard and scanned all the old photos. Now I just need to organize everything and write up some text. I type *true trailblazer* into my first slide, but now I'm questioning my choice of the photo of Great-Gramps digging a foxhole for the first image. Maybe I should start with the photo of him in Italy with his buddies? Or the photo of him in his uniform looking too young to be going off to war?

I move an image of Bisabuelo in his army uniform to the first slide. He was seventeen years old in this photo. Did he know then how much his life would change? That he'd be a great American hero? Or how much his great-grandchildren would love him? Of course, he couldn't have known, but I like thinking about it anyway. Maybe someday, some future child will be looking at my picture and they'll tell their friends, "This is my great-grandmother, Alyssa Velasco. She was a great photographer who won a contest when she was only ten years old."

By the time I've added a few more photos and text, I'm worn out. I crawl to my bed and get under the covers with my clothes still on when I hear Adriana arrive home. When she reaches the top of the stairs, I call out to her.

She pokes her head in my bedroom with Secret in her arms, "What's up, *hermanita*?"

"I want to show you my photo essay for the contest."

"Yay!" she says. I jump down from my bed to grab my laptop off the floor. Adriana sits down on the bed, and I hand it to her.

"How was the movie? Did you go see the scary one about the kids in that Egyptian tomb?"

"No, we should have, but we went to go see something else. It was dumb." She frowns. "But we had fun."

Adriana is suddenly quiet and starts clicking through my presentation. I watch her brown eyes move across each image. Secret paws at the screen, and she pulls him onto her lap to pet. While she views my presentation, I admire how pretty she looks. She has her long hair pinned up into a bun at the top of her head. She's wearing dark blue jeans and a loose white blouse under a pink jacket that I love because it has lots of zippers.

"This is a good start, Allie," she finally says. My heart jumps in my chest. "But are you going to add some original photos?"

I nod. "I'm going to take a picture of Bisa with his Medal of Honor for the ending. Is that good?"

"That'd be cool, but what about a photo of him with his family? Or with his buddies at the GI Forum? This presentation is really heavy on the war. Bisa went to war to ensure his family could have a good life. That's what makes him a trailblazer to me."

I bite down on my lower lip. A boring family picture doesn't sound like any way to win a contest. A photo of him with his WWII Medal of Honor will inspire people and win me the first-place prize. I know it.

"Just think about it," Adriana says. "I'm sure whatever you come up with will be great." She gets up from my bed and hands the laptop back to me.

"Adriana, is that why you're going to Harvard, to be a trailblazer too?"

She winces, and my heart feels like a piñata getting a good whack.

"Harvard is too far away," I say. I can feel tears starting, which I hate because I don't want to look like a baby, but I can't stop.

"Don't cry. C'mon, *hermanita*." Adriana sits next to me again and pulls me close to her. I lay my head against her shoulder. She smells citrusy sweet like grapefruit sprinkled with sugar. She squeezes me tight. "Will you hear me out a little bit?"

I nod.

"The easy thing would be to go to school here, stay at home with all of you . . . that would be so nice. But I've been offered a once-in-a-lifetime opportunity. Harvard, Allie. No one in our family has ever been accepted to an Ivy League school. And no matter how scared I am, I have to go for it because I'm doing this for you and all the kids at the center to show them they can do it too."

"But you don't have to do it for me," I whine. "I want you to stay."

"Oh, Allie." Adriana sighs. "What if Bisabuelo had never gone to war? He did it so that his future family could follow their dreams. Passing on Harvard because I'm afraid or

120

because it'd be easier to stay home would be wasting everything he sacrificed. You understand, right?"

I don't want to admit it, but I do understand. It's like today with the piñata. After several children failed to bust the piñata, one of Victor's little sisters took the stick and bashed a colossal hole into it, sending candy and coins everywhere. She thought it was unfair that by the time she pulled her blindfold off, half the candy was grabbed up by the other kids. Victor and I tried to cheer her up by naming her the great Piñata Buster. "Look at how happy you made the other kids," Victor said to her. "You breaking the piñata made it possible for other kids to have candy." It didn't help. She only stopped pouting when I brought her a bag of leftover candy.

"I understand . . ." I say finally. "You and Bisa are piñata busters. True trailblazers."

"Piñata buster or not, I wouldn't feel right leaving home if you weren't on my side on this. You're my sister, and we'll always be tight no matter where we both go, okay?"

"I'm not going anywhere," I mutter.

"It may not seem like it right now, but I have this feeling that you will travel the world. You'll learn new languages and explore new cultures. I know it, Allie."

I finally smile. "That'd be cool, I guess."

Truth is, I would *love* to travel the world and take photographs. Maybe someday I could work for a magazine and go to Guatemala and take pictures of the real *volcán de Fuego*. I could visit the towns in North Africa and Italy where my *bisabuelo* served during the war. I could interview Junko Tabei and take her picture with that crazy pickax.

"Can I ask you a favor, Adriana? It's about Victor."

"Victor Garcia, the tutor?"

"Yes, he's applied to Bishop Crest Middle but hasn't heard back yet. Do you think you could write a letter of recommendation for him? He's not from here and doesn't have the connections most Sendak kids have. A recommendation from you would really help. Please."

"Of course. Victor's a great kid. I had no idea he was applying to Bishop. I'll write a letter tomorrow. No problem."

"Victor will be the first in his family to graduate from high school someday, but first he needs to get into Bishop Crest. If he could get in, then he'd just have to find the money . . ." I trail off, thinking. "Maybe if I win the contest I can give him the two-hundred-dollar prize money. That would help a little, right?"

"You would give up the prize money for him? You must really like him. Is he your crush? Wooo wooo wooo!" Adriana makes playful sirens sounds. It's the sound we both make when we know people have crushes.

My face feels hot. "I don't care about the prize money. I want to be the first Velasco to win this contest, and I want the trophy for our shelf. That'd be nice. I'm tired of being the only one without something."

Adriana kisses my head. "I know that bothers you, but you know what, Allie? The real rewards you can't put on a shelf. Remember?"

"Bisa always tells me that, but—"

"No buts, it's true in more ways than you even know right now." She turns off the light as she leaves. "Good night, Allie. Tomorrow is another day full of opportunities for epic greatness."

My room is dark, but I feel a warm golden light twinkling inside me. I hope she's right. So far, this school year has been a bust. I could use a day of epic greatness.

Chapter 16

I know it's a long shot, but on Monday morning, I go ahead and pull out two different colored socks from my sock drawer to wear with two different colored pairs of Keds. This used to be Sara and my April Fool's Day tradition. We came up with it in third grade. We'd both wear mismatched socks and shoes all day. For a second, I worry that if she isn't wearing mismatched socks and shoes, I'll look like a dork. I shake off that thought. It's our tradition, and I can do it if I want.

When I get downstairs for a quick bowl of cereal, Ava and Aiden are already diving into cornflakes. They look innocent, but I know better. I grab the box of cereal from the counter and inspect it carefully to make sure that the sugary cornflakes haven't been replaced with Secret's cat food. I shift the box left to right and back and forth to spot any fake spiders or roaches thrown in there.

"What are you doing?" Aiden shakes his head.

I shrug. "Just checking."

"For what? A little toy prize at the bottom? Aren't you a little old for that?"

Ava snorts.

"It's April Fool's Day," I say, and glare at him. I sniff the box some more. "I'm not falling for any of your tricks."

"The cereal is fine. Look, we're eating it." Ava shovels a big scoop in her mouth.

I go ahead and pour a bowl of cereal. I taste a cornflake. It's good. I grab the carton of milk and pour. Aiden bursts into howling laughter, and Ava giggles like an evil demon child.

"Augh!" I shriek. I've just poured orange juice over my cereal. "You switched it!"

"April Fool's!" they both shout.

All I can do is call them creeps and put the cereal out for Secret, but even he snubs it and struts off. I can't believe I fell for the old switch-the-milk trick. I should know better. I pour myself another bowl, and this time, I grab a pitcher out of the fridge. I check it. It's milk.

When Mom and Dad come into the kitchen, I want to warn them, but Aiden gives me one of those big brother don't-you-dare looks and I shut up.

Mom grabs the milk carton, ready to pour some into her coffee. Aiden and Ava exchange deliriously happy smiles. Sickos.

"You kids are being awfully quiet this morning," she says. She is two seconds from pouring orange juice into her coffee, when Dad jumps in, like the good firefighter he is, to save the day. He takes it from her.

"Better check that first, sweetie. Don't forget it's April Fool's Day." He eyes the inside of the carton. "Just as I suspected . . ." He pours a glass of orange juice. "Nice try, Aiden."

Mom shakes her head. "You almost got me." She pours milk into her coffee. "Please be careful with the pranks today, kids. Especially you, Aiden . . ."

Aiden lets out an exasperated protest.

"Don't act innocent, Aiden. I don't want to be called into the principal's office for any antics that go wrong, okay?"

"It would be very uncool for your mom, best news anchor

for the fourth year in a row, to be called into the office today," Dad says, holding the trophy over his head.

"You won again!" Ava squeals. We all rush and give her a group hug.

"Okay, I won't do anything nutso today," Aiden says, dropping a handful of very realistic rubbery spiders and roaches onto the kitchen counter.

"I cannot make that same promise!" Ava says, dangling a Ziploc bag full of Oreos filled with toothpaste. She'll offer them to the boys in her class. Even with their mouths full of thick, minty paste, they'll still adore her.

"Please try to be nice to the boys in your class," Dad says.

"No promises on April Fool's Day!" Ava giggles. "It's my April Rules Day."

Sendak Elementary is famous for its April Fool's Day. Everyone, even the cafeteria cooks and the librarian, get into the act—but the teachers are the worst! It's the one day that teachers get payback for all the whining their students have done all year. I've survived all their best pranks by learning not to trust anything they say on April 1.

Last year, our teacher gave us a word search in English class. He said that if the entire class completed it in fifteen minutes, he'd let everyone out of school a full hour early. He handed out a sheet of paper with vocabulary words that didn't exist anywhere in the word search. All of us were sweating it out, while the timer ticked away. Our teacher read the paper and sipped coffee while we suffered.

For that reason, I don't trust any teachers on April Fool's Day. The end-of-the-year field trip isn't canceled. There isn't a math test today that's worth 99 percent of our grade. Pizza made with worm toppings is not today's lunch special. It's all one big April Fool's prank.

So when Mrs. Wendy announced that we're going to present our contest entries in front of the class for helpful feedback, I wasn't falling for it. There's no way I'm ready. And what does she mean by helpful feedback? It's April Fool's Day. If she doesn't like what she hears, will she pelt us with worm toppings?

I look around the class. Is anyone going to take her up on her offer? Sara looks back at her guitar. Grace walks up to the front of the classroom. "I'm submitting a poem in honor of my mom, a true trailblazer," she says. "She is raising me all by herself this year, and I admire her for starting her own business."

Grace's poem is long and rhyming. When she's done, everyone claps as she takes her seat.

"Positive feedback for Grace?" Mrs. Wendy calls out. I raise my hand.

"It rhymed well," I start. "And it really shows that you love your mom."

Grace turns in her seat and smiles at me. Haley raises her hand next. She always has to copy whatever I do. She's been that way since second grade. Isn't it enough that she copied my best friend? You've won, Hayley. You can stop already.

"I liked it, but it seemed too long," she says. "Mrs. Wendy, isn't there a rule that poems can only be twenty lines?"

"Good feedback. It seemed a bit long to me as well. If you go over twenty lines you'll be disqualified. Please double-check." Grace looks down at her paper and starts to count.

"Anyone else?"

Several hands go up including Sara's, but Mrs. Wendy picks Ethan. He doesn't have his photo presentation ready, but he puts up one single photo of Principal Vihn.

When he's done talking about how Principal Vihn emigrated from Vietnam to America when he was just a baby, Ethan shrugs. "I'm going to add more to it."

"It's due tomorrow. You need to get to it," says Mrs. Wendy.

No one else has any more tips for him, so she calls on Sara. Sara jumps up, grabs her guitar, and takes a seat in the front of the classroom. She's wearing matching shoes. A pang of hurt shoots through me. Did she forget about our tradition? Or maybe she doesn't care anymore. Maybe there is no hope that we'll ever be best friends again. I don't know why I'm shocked. I just am. I kept hoping she would wear mismatched socks and shoes . . . especially after she reminded me of April Fool's Day. I wonder if I can call Dad and have him bring me another pair at lunch?

"My song is titled, 'American Dream.' It is dedicated to Rocky Velasco, World War II veteran and Medal of Honor recipient," Sara says. "I wrote this song *corrido*-style, which is a Mexican folk style of music. For the contest, it can't be any longer than three minutes. Hope you like it.

"Gather around young and old,
I have a story that must be told.
About a young soldier who went off to war
To add his muscle to the fight,
Knowing he may never see his family again,
He battles forward with all his might.

"The great soldier won't say he's a hero,
Though he fought for the land of the free.
His sacrifice was for everyone,

Especially for you and me,
Especially for you and me.

"Leaving his mother and brother behind,
He knows that duty calls.
Fighting far away in Europe,
The American dream must never fall.
In the battle, the young soldier learns
To never stop to cry.
He must move on without his fallen brothers,
Though the pain will never die.

"The great soldier won't say he's a hero,
Though he fought for the land of the free.
His sacrifice was for everyone,
Especially for you and me,
Especially for you and me."

As soon as she finishes, everyone claps. Mrs. Wendy gives
Sara a standing ovation from her desk.

Really? Is this some kind of April Fool's joke? I have to
admit it has a nice melody, but standing-ovation worthy? I
look over at Victor. He's clapping too.

Of course, Hayley is the first to raise her hand. "I think it's awesome. I'm sure it will win."

A few more kids gush about how the song made them tap their feet, or how the words made them feel grateful . . . blah blah blah. I'm staring down at my cell phone looking for a photo I can present, when Mrs. Wendy calls my name.

"Alyssa? What did you think? After all, it's a song dedicated to your great-grandfather."

Yep. I'm perfectly aware that Sara has chosen to write a poem about my *bisabuelo* for the Trailblazer contest. Been there. Still dealing with it.

"It would be helpful," Sara says sweetly.

All of sudden, I feel everyone's eyes on me. While everyone waits for my response, Sara bends down to fold her jeans up at her ankles to show her socks. One is lavender, and the other is a bright pink-and-orange-striped sock. She's wearing mismatched socks! She didn't forget! She smiles at me. Now I don't feel like such a dork with my mismatched socks and shoes. I smile back.

"I think it's good," I say finally. Sara takes her seat but glances over at me one more time. Is this a sign that we'll be best friends again?

"Good, Alyssa. Would you like to present your project?"

Augh! If I don't stand up with something, I'll look like a scaredy-cat. Still, I have nothing. I grab my cell phone and shuffle up to the front of the class.

My throat feels dry, and my palms are getting moist. It's April Fool's Day, I think. I have an idea. No introduction. I go straight into it.

"Violets are orange and red,
Roses are gray and cool,
I'm not done with my project yet,
So Happy April Fool's!"

Chapter 17

I'm still thinking about Sara wearing mismatched socks when something strange and awesome happens at lunchtime— and I don't mean the April Fool's lunch special of French bread pizza with worm toppings, which is really chopped pepperoni and onions. I sit down at the usual table and Sara sits down next to me.

"Worm toppings! Yum!" she says, and nudges me playfully with her elbow. Usually, Victor sits next to me, but I am so happy, I don't say anything.

"Did you get some sour lemonade?" I ask her.

"Yep. Is it really sour?"

We both take a quick sip and scrunch up our faces until we both laugh. It is super sour, but good. It's just like last year until Hayley takes the seat across from me. Is this some sort of April Fool's Day joke?

Victor plops down next to Hayley. "What's up, Hays?"

"Don't call me that!" she yells at him.

I giggle and am surprised when Sara laughs too. "Allie, thanks for the nice words about my song," Sara says.

"It was good. And I like your socks," I say.

Principal Vihn is suddenly speaking over the intercom. He announces in a very serious tone that the library will be closed this afternoon due to a worm infestation.

"Apparently, some of the worms from your pizza escaped to the library and have made new homes inside of the books."

A bunch of us groan because Principal Vihn is the biggest April Fool's prankster ever! Every year he comes up with something crazy.

"And don't forget, starting after lunch all students will have GPS chips inserted into your noses so we know where you're at all the time. The only drawback is that you must refrain from sneezing for the rest of the school year. Teachers will be confiscating all tissue boxes in the classroom. Remember, no sneezing! Good luck!"

"This school is *loco!*" Victor exclaims and claps. "At my old school in San Antonio, they weren't down with any pranks. They'd call our parents if we even mentioned April Fool's."

"Speaking of April's Fool's Day . . ." says Hayley. "Did you see that Sara and I were wearing mismatched socks?"

My stomach twists and turns.

She pulls her feet up to the chair and rolls up her jeans. "See?"

She also has one lavender sock and one pink-and-orange-striped sock on. The same mismatched socks as Sara. How dare Sara share our tradition with Hayley! If they're going to be best buddies now, they should start their own stupid tradition.

"Look at mine," I snap. I pull my jeans up to show my mismatched shoes and socks. "This has been Sara and my tradition since third grade. You're just a big copycat, Hayley!" I push away from the table and glower at her shocked face.

"Why would I want to copy you?" Hayley says. "There's nothing you do that's worth copying."

"Hayley, stop!" Sara says.

"Tell that to your mismatched socks! And, Sara, don't bother. You don't really care about making a tribute to my *bisabuelo,* anyway. You just want to win—"

136

"That's not true!" she says.

"Whatever! There's no way you're taking first with that dumb song anyway!" I can't stop myself from continuing. "My great-gramps is going to be so embarrassed by your *corrido*."

Sara's mouth drops open.

"Allie," Victor says softly. Sara looks like she wants to cry, but I have a whole bunch more to get off my chest.

"A friend doesn't sabotage another friend's chances of winning a contest. Even if they aren't talking anymore. You know how much winning this trophy means to me, and you're trying to wreck it on purpose."

"Allie," Victor tries again.

"Victor wants me to win and doesn't try to compete with me. If you stopped trying so hard to become Hayley, you'd realize what true friendship looks like." I gesture wildly at Victor. He doesn't meet my eyes.

I don't bother to pick up my lunch tray as I get up and stomp out of the cafeteria. April Fool's Day or not, I'm tired of being Sara's fool. One day, she's a fuzzy kitten and then the next day she's a snake. We will never be best friends again. I take off the bracelet she made me last year and throw it into a trash can on the way to the nurse's office.

Chapter 18

Within twenty minutes, my dad picks me up at school. Cinder, the firehouse dog, is in the backseat, which calms me down. I pet Cinder, and she licks my entire face.

"You sounded angry on the phone so I thought seeing Cinder would cheer you up," he says. "Is everything going okay with school? Was the contest deadline today?"

"No, it's tomorrow." I mumble between Cinder's kisses. I remember the day my dad and the rest of the guys from the firehouse adopted Cinder from the animal shelter. My dad was so excited. After school, Adriana drove all of us to the station to meet the young Rottweiler who had a ripped ear and tail. My dad said the shelter had tons of cats there for adoption, so Sara and I went with my mom to check it out and we ended up adopting Secret. The shelter staff asked us if we would change Secret's name, but Sara and I agreed it was the perfect name for such a fluffy, shy kitten. It's memories like these I have to push away now. It's over for Sara and me. I've lost my best friend for good, but at least I still have Secret.

"Do you want to talk about it? Are you stressing out? I know how you get with these contests. Is there anything I can do to help?"

I shake my head. "It's almost finished. I just have to take a picture of Bisa with his medal. Then I'll be done."

"Whoa! That's a photo I'd like to see. He's always so mysterious about that medal. I can't remember the last time I've seen it."

I nod. I'm trying to listen to my dad, but honestly, my mind is back at school. I didn't even say good-bye to Victor. I feel bad about that. Twice, he called my name. Maybe he thought I was being too rough on Sara, but I wasn't. Sara deserved it. I'll call him tonight.

"Sorry you're not feeling well, kiddo. I called Bisabuelo. He's at the GI Forum helping out. I'll take you there and then you can go home with him. He'll make you some *manzanilla* tea."

"Thanks." Whenever one of us is sick on a school day, we always go over to Bisabuelo's house because he's usually home. If he's not, he's at the GI Forum hanging out with other war vets. I've gone with him to the GI Forum several times, and it's always fun. They have a refrigerator full of root beer, a pool table, and two big flat-screen TVs.

Over the years, the veterans have gotten younger and younger. There aren't too many WWII veterans hanging out there anymore. Bisabuelo says all his brothers are "passing on." I know that he means that they're dying, but he likes to say "passing on." I don't want to even THINK about Bisabuelo passing on.

The few WWII and Korean War vets there have known my *bisabuelo* a long time, and they like to talk politics and use their own vocabulary. Last year, I heard one of them call our new mayor a "whippersnapper" because he thought he was too young, inexperienced, and cocky. I told Sara about that, and for an entire week, she went around calling the boys in our class "whippersnappers." It was hilarious. But that was then. Now, I don't think anything she does is hilarious. She's the "whippersnapper" now.

Once Dad has pulled up at the curb in front of the center, Bisa is already there. He comes over and opens the car door for me. "*¿Qué pasó*, Allie? How do you feel, *mija*?"

"Not so good," I say softly. I kiss Cinder good-bye. My *bisabuelo* grabs my book bag for me, but before we leave to go inside, he gives my dad a hug and kiss. Bisabuelo always says that no matter how big firefighters are, they still need kisses and hugs from their *abuelos*. And the way my dad hugs back and smiles, I know it's the truth. I don't think I'll ever be too old for hugs and kisses either.

My *bisabuelo* locks arms with me and guides me into the GI Forum the way I imagine he probably helped injured soldiers get off the battlefield. Once we're inside the center, he introduces me to a bunch of the guys and settles me onto a couch in front of a television.

"I'm just going to finish up some things, and we'll be on our way in a jiffy." Bisa kisses my head and rushes off to the center's office. I'm surrounded by walls covered with photos of veterans from every war . . . WWII, Vietnam, Korea, Iraq, and Afghanistan. There are also Prisoner of War banners that say *You are not forgotten* and framed medals with different color ribbons. I take my camera and start snapping some shots. These medals will look good in my project.

My *bisabuelo* puts a hand on my shoulder. "Some great stuff here, eh?"

I nod. "So many awards!" I squeal. "I hope it's okay if I took some photos of the walls with all the medals and banners."

"You're feeling better, eh?"

I bite down on my lip. Time to confess the truth. "I'm not really *sick* sick," I say. "It's just school stuff and I didn't want to be there."

"What happened, *mija*? Was someone bullying you?"

"No, nothing like that. It's just stuff with Sara. She's still being a jerk."

"*Mija*, school is important. You can't just quit when it's tough. You don't want to make walking away when things get hard a habit."

I know I'm being a big baby, but I can't help it. Today was just a bad day. "I'll make it up by working on my project, okay?" I'm relieved when Bisabuelo puts his arm around me. I never want to disappoint my great-gramps.

I point up at a picture of two young men standing on top of a tank. "This one is from the Korean War. Are there any guys here today from that war?"

Bisa looks around the room. "Yep, Auggie over there, the one playing pool. Good guy. The young man next to him is

Michael. He served in Afghanistan. He has the best singing voice. We keep telling him to try out for one of those singing shows on TV. He could win."

"Do you think they would mind if I took photos of them?"

"Everyone is *familia* here. Why not?"

I follow my *bisabuelo* to the pool table. "Brothers, my great-granddaughter would like to take some photos of you, would that be okay? Maybe she'll use them in her school project, and we'll all be famous!"

Everyone laughs and makes comments like, "Not as famous as you, Rocky!"

As I take one photo after another, I notice that everyone wants a photo with my *bisabuelo*. They put their arms around him. In return, he is quick with kind words and hugs. Everyone is so nice. No one even makes fun of the fact that I'm wearing mismatched shoes.

As Great-Gramps drives us home, I realize that the whole time I was with him at the center I forgot about dumb Sara and Hayley.

When we get to his house, all I can think of is seeing Bisa's Medal of Honor. He puts on a kettle of hot water and then goes downstairs to "dig it up." Sara may have her silly little song, but I'll have this photo. This will be my chance to blaze my trail to the top of the contest like Junko on Mount Everest. I'll leave Sara behind once and for all. After all, no one can resist a hero with a great medal. Don't all the best movies end that way? The underdog hockey team rallies to win the championship trophy. The daring space warrior gets a medal draped around her neck for saving the universe. The orphan prince gets his shiny crown at the end. It's the perfect ending for my presentation too. My secret weapon for the first-place prize!

Bisa comes into the living room with a wooden box. Chills run through me. It's the medal I've heard about all my life and never seen. I guide Bisa where to sit. "Okay, so I'm thinking you sit here on your chair. With the window behind me, we'll have perfect lighting." Bisa takes his seat, still holding the wooden case in his hands. I pull the sheer drapes across the window to give the setting a golden glow, a tip I learned on a photography blog. "You'll open the box and I'll snap a bunch of shots. Just look natural. Ready?"

He nods. I take a deep breath, hold the camera up, and focus it. He opens the box slowly, I zoom in, but the box is empty. I blink rapidly and look again, but there's still nothing where the Medal of Honor should be. No sky-blue ribbon. No shiny, star-shaped award.

"Bisa, where is your medal?" I gasp.

chapter 19

I lower my camera, half expecting Bisa to yell, "April Fool's!" but he doesn't. He pulls a photo out of the box instead.

"Bisa, please tell me this is some sort of joke," I say. "You have the medal, right? Did it fall out on the stairs?" My face is turning hotter the longer he stays silent. My heart beats fast.

He shakes his head. "I'm sorry to disappoint you, *mija*, but I gave the award away a long time ago."

What? "W-why would you do that?" I stammer. Who could he possibly have given it to? If my parents find out about this, they will flip out. "Do Mom and Dad know?"

"Nope! Only you know and maybe some of the guys at the Forum," he says. I slump down on the couch. I don't want to be first in our family to know because I don't want any of this to be true. What about my picture for my project? What am I going to do now?

"Who did you give it to?" I wonder briefly if there's a way to get it back.

"You know why I won the award, right?" he asks.

I nod. The story of my *bisabuelo*'s heroics during a battle in Italy was described in the documentary and in the newspapers. Every single Veterans or Memorial Day, the governor or mayor invites him to speak about how he took down a nest of machine guns, but my *bisa* isn't comfortable talking about it. He says it sounds too much like he's bragging. He doesn't believe in bragging. Instead he likes to tell stories about the soldiers he knew and the many ways people can help veterans coming home. Everyone enjoys his stories.

"Well, after the documentary was released, one of the grandchildren of a man in my unit looked me up. His grandfather was Olin Baxter. Anyway, he came all the way from Loganville, Georgia, to visit me. He'd seen the documentary and wanted to meet the man that served with his grandpa. Olin was one of the best men I ever knew. He was a brother to me, so I gave the medal to his grandson. This is a picture of Olin and me during the war."

"Oh, Bisa . . ." I ignore the photo and instead bury my face into my hands. My secret weapon against Sara is *poof,* gone. "The president gave it to you. I can't believe you gave it away."

Bisabuelo shakes his head. "I won that award doing what any other soldier would have done in my same situation. His grandpa, on the other hand, made the ultimate sacrifice."

I know that means Olin died, but disappointment bubbles up inside me. "This is so not fair," I say. "Here I am trying to get an award to put on the family shelf and you're giving them away!"

Great-Gramps puts the photo of Olin back into the box. He closes it gently. "*Mija,* that medal was never mine. I always felt like it belonged to the men who died. For me, giving it to Olin's grandson was the right thing to do."

"What do I do now?" I say. "You holding the medal was going to be my winning shot."

"I'm sorry, *mija*, I didn't realize how important having a photo of me and my medal would be to your contest. My apologies, *mija*, but I hope you'll understand."

No, I don't understand. I'll never understand.

"Let's take one more photo anyway," Bisa says. He sits forward with the medal-less box cradled in his hands, ready for the picture to be taken. He waits for me. I don't really feel like taking the photo anymore. How will I ever win this contest now?

"What's the point?" I say.

"Please, for me, Allie." The lighting from the living room window casts a golden glow around his face. I step forward and raise the camera to take a few pictures. The only thing that would make the photo more perfect is if he had the actual medal in his hands. This feels like an icy cold avalanche just as I reached the mountain peak. All is lost. I look down at my mismatched shoes and socks and want to cry. Stupid shoes. Stupid tradition. Stupid medal. Stupid contest. Stupid me.

Chapter 20

"Now if you haven't already done so, please double-check your subject line," says Mrs. Wendy. She hovers over us in the computer lab. Most of the class has already submitted their contest entries from home, but there are still a few like me who need to submit it today.

Mrs. Wendy seems more nervous than all of us put together. She thinks we're going to mess up a submission rule and be disqualified. I know the submission instructions forward and backward. I'm not about to lose this contest to

Sara because I didn't use the correct online application or proper subject line. No way!

Victor is sitting in the reading lounge with Ethan and Diego. I never got a chance to call him last night. I was feeling too bummed about Bisa giving away his beautiful medal. I didn't feel like talking to anyone. Even Secret could see I didn't want company last night. He hung out for a while with me in my bedroom and then moved on to Aiden's room. Cats hate being ignored.

Sara is in the computer room five seats down from me. Hayley is helping her submit her entry. A few days ago, seeing them together laughing and helping each other would have hurt my feelings, but now I could care less. Who needs her anyway?

My presentation is done. And even without the photo I wanted of Great-Gramps with his medal, I think it will beat Sara's song. I started it with a photo of Great-Gramps as a young soldier and ended it with the image of him receiving the Medal of Honor from President Truman. It's a photo from the newspaper. It's not the secret-weapon shot I wanted so badly, but hopefully it'll be enough to win. My entire reputation at Sendak and as a Velasco is riding on this contest.

Victor takes the seat next to me. "You've already submitted your photo essay?"

"I'm about to. I just need to click submit."

"Hurry up so you can sit with me in the reading lounge. Mrs. Wendy said that if we're not submitting contest entries today, we could hang out there and read whatever we wanted. Diego found a new comic book series about zombie cats."

"Zombie cats?" I look around and catch Diego and Ethan watching me from across the library. When they see I notice them, they turn away. "Is everyone talking about me and what I said to Sara yesterday at lunch?"

"Sort of, but it's no big deal. Everyone thinks Hayley started it because . . . well, she sort of starts everything, right?"

I let out a sigh of relief. "I wanted to say sorry for not saying good-bye to you yesterday after everything. I felt bad about leaving my tray and stomping off."

Victor shrugs. "No worries, Allie, but Sara was really upset. Grace told me that Sara was thinking of not submitting her song for the contest, but I guess she's decided to do it after all." He glances over at Sara and Hayley.

My heart drops into my stomach and twists around.

"Is there any way you two can make up and talk it over?"

I shake my head. "I don't think so. Maybe I'm being a Miss Prissy-Pants, but she's being a Miss Prissy-Butt."

"Does Miss Prissy-Pants want to hurry up and click submit so we can go read about zombie cats?"

"As long as one of those zombie cats isn't named Secret," I say. Victor chuckles.

I face the screen. With one click, my contest entry form is sent. With one click, I could make Sendak history. With one click, I could finally win first place and have a glorious trophy for the family trophy shelf.

"Hurry up already," Victor urges.

I click my mouse and away my project goes. Now all I can do is read about zombie cats—and wait.

Chapter 21

Today, Mrs. Wendy says that she's "completely had it" with all of us asking her about the Trailblazer contest. On the contest webpage it says that finalists will be posted on April 12, but today is April 12 and there is no information.

Mrs. Wendy throws her hands up. "We'll know when we know."

It's hard for me to focus on anything else but the contest results. How can I focus on math, spelling, history, or science when I know there's a panel of judges out there deciding my fate? According to the website, the judges award points for each project based on how well you addressed the trail-blazer theme, originality, creativity, and imagery. I hope I've racked up points galore!

"But when will we know?" Grace whines. "I'll need to get the awards ceremony on my dad's schedule. He's really busy and needs advance notice or he can't attend."

"The ceremony is only for the finalists, right, Mrs. Wendy?" Hayley asks.

"Only the finalists are required to present their work in front of an audience," says Mrs. Wendy.

"See, Grace, you won't have to worry your dad about it," says Hayley.

"Burn!" Diego exclaims. The whole class erupts into laughs, and Mrs. Wendy lets out a long sigh and shakes her head. You can tell she's ready for summer break. Grace slumps down in her chair.

"That's not cool, Hayley." I glare back at her. "Grace's poem could win. At least she entered the contest. You didn't even bother to try."

I glare at Diego too. Not nice, dude.

Hayley rolls her eyes at me. I give Sara a disappointed look. She looks down quickly and picks at her nails. The chipped orange polish looks like ripped construction paper.

The old Sara would never have tolerated rudeness like Hayley's.

"Thanks, Allie," Grace says over her shoulder to me.

"You're welcome," I say.

Principal Vihn shows up at the classroom door and speaks to Mrs. Wendy.

"Allie, Principal Vihn needs to speak to you. Please grab your things," Mrs. Wendy says.

Is it about the contest? Did I make it as a finalist? But then why do I have to grab my things? Everyone watches me while I gather my stuff into my book bag. I have a very bad feeling about this. Victor gives me a puzzled look. I shrug and mouth, "No idea."

"I hope everything is okay, Allie," Grace whispers as I pass her. I smile and nod.

Outside the classroom, Principal Vihn apologizes for taking me out of class and explains that my mom is coming to pick up Ava and me. This is not good. Something bad has happened if Mom is leaving work. Award-winning reporters never leave work early unless it's to be the first to break a juicy news story.

"Is everything okay?" I ask him.

"I think everything will be fine, but it's best you talk to

your mom, sweetheart," says Principal Vihn. "I'm sorry I can't tell you more. You know I would if I could."

I smile back at him. Principal Vihn is always nice like that.

Ava shows up to the office at the same time and surprises me when she takes my hand. She is on the verge of tears. "What's going on?" she asks. We enter the office, and Principal Vihn tells us to take a seat while we wait for Mom.

Ava and I look around the office. She points up to the photo of Adriana on the wall. "Look how pretty she looks, Allie," she says.

In the photo, Adriana holds the Mayor's Youth Power Award. She looks beautiful. Next to her framed picture is a photograph of Carmen Eberhart, the first female student enrolled at Sendak Elementary. Our school was an all-boys school until 1984. In the photo, Carmen is standing outside the front of the school in a pretty dress. Whenever I'm in Principal Vihn's office, I always nod in respect to her. I just feel like I should. I bet she had a hard time being one of the first few girls to attend Sendak. Boys can be such dweebs. Imagine being outnumbered by a bunch of Aidens, Diegos, and Ethans. Poor girl! She had it rough, I'm sure.

Principal Vihn notices that I'm staring at Carmen's

picture. "Our first female Sendak student. She lives in Washington, DC, now," he says. "Works at the Pentagon."

Wow. Ambitious much? There's no way my picture will ever hang on the wall with this kind of competition. Suddenly, Mom comes in and hugs us. "Good, you girls are here."

"What's going on?" I ask.

"Bisabuelo collapsed at the GI Forum today. Your dad is at the hospital with him."

Ava covers her face with her hands and immediately starts to whimper. Mom kisses her on the head. "I'm just going to sign you girls out, and then we'll go visit him." She strokes Ava's hair and then heads over to Principal Vihn. "Allie, help your sister get ready to go."

I hear my mom's voice, but I can't move. Collapsed? What does that mean? "Allie, Ava needs your help," my mom says as she finishes up with Principal Vihn.

I snap into action. While Ava cries, I help her put on her yellow sweater one arm at a time, like how I used to when she was little.

"Let's go, Ava," I say softly to her. She takes my hand again and squeezes it tight.

At the hospital, Adriana, Aiden, and my dad are sitting at Bisabuelo's bedside. There are at least a dozen wires and tubes sticking out of him that are hooked up to beeping, blinking machines. I ignore everyone's puffy red eyes and sad faces and move closer to Bisabuelo.

"He's going to be fine, right?" I say. I lean in to kiss his cheek and whisper to him, "You have to be fine, Bisabuelo. We need you."

Ava bursts into tears. Adriana takes her and pulls her onto her lap. Dad gestures to all of us to follow him outside.

"I don't want to leave him," Aiden says.

"He needs his rest, and we need to talk." Dad puts his arms around Aiden's sunken shoulders.

In the hallway, all of us huddle close together.

"The doctor says that the cough he's had for a while is actually a chest infection. Luckily, Bisabuelo was at the GI Forum when he passed out, and they were able to get help fast. They're going to keep him here for a few days just to make sure there are no complications and then he'll get to come home with us, okay?" Dad says. "Mom and I've decided he should stay with us from now on."

All of us nod. This is good news. Bisa should be at home with us where we can keep a closer eye on him.

"For now, we should all hang around. It'd be nice if he wakes up and we're all here. Don't you think?" says Mom. All of us nod some more.

Mom and Adriana rush off to buy juice and chips for us, and the rest of us go back to his room and watch him breathe. Sometime he winces like he's in pain, but he doesn't wake up.

"The tubes are hurting him," Aiden says. "Can't we do anything?"

"He's probably just dreaming. He's always slept rough," Dad says. "When I was a kid and I'd stay over at his house, he'd sometimes wake up from bad dreams about the war."

Is that what he's doing? Dreaming about the war? About Olin Baxter? At that moment, I want to hug Bisabuelo. I feel horrible for pressuring him about the medal.

"Dad, why did Bisa get sick?"

"Well, Bisabuelo is getting old, Alyssa. He's more vulnerable to things like infections. We don't like to admit it because he seems so strong, but his health is fragile." My dad pulls me close to him and kisses my head. "Don't worry. We're going to take good care of him."

I nod, but I can't help but worry. Could Bisa have gotten ill because I stressed him out about needing a photo of his medal for my contest?

"You don't think it was caused by stress or something?" I ask.

"Has Bisa been stressed out, lately? I haven't noticed. Did he say something to you?"

"No, not really. I was just wondering," I say. I don't want to tell him what I know about the medal.

My parents don't know that Bisa doesn't have it anymore. They don't know that I was so upset about it. I haven't told them anything. I hold back tears. Lying motionless in his hospital bed, Great-Gramps no longer seems ninety-one years old to me.

Instead, I see the young boy who stood outside of the school with his mom hoping to be accepted. I see the brave teenager who volunteered to go to war. I see the young soldier who risked his life in battle to save others. I get up from dad's lap. I touch Bisa's hand and give him another kiss on the cheek.

"You're safe here with us, Bisabuelo," I whisper. "You're safe and sound."

Chapter 22

It's early evening when Bisabuelo opens his eyes. We're all so grateful. The nurse and doctor come in and shoo everyone except Dad from the room. They've promised us that we will get to visit with him, but for now we're ushered into the waiting room. Aiden and Ava are playing card games on the floor. I can tell that this trip to the hospital has affected them. Ava hasn't thrown the cards in a defeated tantrum. Aiden hasn't stormed off. Neither of them care if they lose to each other today. Mom and Adriana are fielding phone calls from family. Everyone is worried and wants to fly in to see Bisabuelo.

Suddenly Sara is standing in front of me with a bouquet of yellow flowers.

"Hey, Allie," she says. Her mom and dad are behind her holding a brown paper sack.

"Oh, Alyssa! How you holding up, kiddo?" Sara's mom hugs me. My mom and Adriana get off the phone and greet them with long hugs.

"It's so nice of you guys to come," Adriana says.

"Well, Sara told us how Alyssa got called out of class, so I called your mom and she told me the news," says Sara's mom. "The least we could do is stop by and bring you some dinner. Hope everyone likes gyros."

Sara's dad places the brown sack of gyros on the small table in the waiting room.

"Thanks!" Aiden exclaims, and dives into the bags with Ava. I don't have an appetite at all, but I admit the gyros smell delicious.

"Hey, it's the Lopez clan!" My dad exclaims, coming around the corner with the doctor. Everyone exchanges more hugs. My dad is so happy to see his friends. Sara keeps passing me sympathetic smiles and I know I should smile back, but right now I'm not in the mood. I'm still not talking to her no matter how many gyros and yellow flowers she brings.

"Bisa is awake and alert, so we can go and see him now. Your timing is perfect!" Dad says to them. We pick up our things and head to the room, but I feel a tap on my shoulder.

"Allie, I need to talk to you about something," Sara whispers.

"Right now? Bisabuelo just woke up. I have to go."

"It'll be quick. I'm sorry that I shared our April Fool's tradition with Hayley."

I shrug. "I'm over it," I say even though I'm really not.

"I came to school with the mismatched socks and shoes, but I didn't put them on right away. I was worried you had forgotten our tradition so I didn't want to look like a total freak. Things haven't been the same for us since after Christmas . . ."

Tell me about it.

"But once I got to school, I changed into the socks before class started. When Hayley saw me changing my socks, she nagged me to let her have the other pair. I wasn't trying to disrespect our tradition."

"Okay, fine," I say to her. I'm still mad at her for not talking to me this semester, for choosing Hayley over me, for not wearing the bracelet I made her anymore, and for entering the contest using my *bisabuelo* as her subject.

"When I saw you were wearing mismatched shoes and socks, I was so happy, but I didn't realize how mad you'd get if Hayley had on the socks too."

"Okay. You didn't know. I gotta go now." I turn to leave, but she calls out for me again.

"There's something else." She picks at one of her painted fingernails. The old best friend Allie would have told her to stop. That's Hayley's job now. What do I care if she picks her nails until she's ruined them? "About the contest . . . if I win, I'm going to donate the prize money to the GI Forum's wounded veteran's fund in honor of your *bisabuelo*. I won't keep a cent. Not even for a shopping spree."

I stare down at the tile floor. It's nice that she wants to donate the money to the wounded veteran's fund, but then I do a replay of what she just said. She sure is confident that she'll be named a finalist. I mean, she's already talking about winning the whole shebang and donating prize money. That's bold.

"Why are you so sure that you're going to be a finalist?" I ask.

"You didn't hear?" She stops and then shakes her head. "Oh, maybe you were gone already . . . You and I are finalists. We made it. Next week, we get to present for first place."

"I'm a finalist?"

"They announced it this afternoon at school. Mrs. Wendy ran around hugging everyone. She was so happy. She says there's never been three finalists from Sendak before."

"I have to tell Bisa," I turn to rush into Bisabuelo's room with the best news. Wait! I stop in my tracks. Three finalists?

"Did Grace make it too?" I ask.

"No, it's Victor. I didn't even know he was submitting anything. Did you?"

"Victor? Victor Garcia?" I stand there stunned. Sara nods. This can't be right. I bite down on my lip. Surely, he would have told me. All this time, we've been talking about the contest and he's been helping me. Why didn't he tell me he entered the contest?

ChapteR 23

Victor Garcia calls my name in the hallway, but I pretend he's calling another Allie somewhere. Although I know that's not possible. There's only one Allie at Sendak. At least I've got that going for me.

I ignore him and keep walking to my classroom. He should have told me he was entering the Trailblazer contest. This whole time I thought he wanted me to win, but now he's a finalist too. It's probably another plot to sabotage me. He's done it before! I should have walked away at the science fair and never talked to Victor Garcia.

At the lunch table, he takes the seat across from me. He looks like a sad puppy, but I won't give in. Everyone is watching us because Sendak is full of nosy-butts. For a minute, I stand and consider sitting somewhere else, but why should I go? I've been at Sendak for five years now. Victor is the newbie that should leave and find a new seat.

"Allie, I never expected to be a finalist. I was only entering the contest for the extra credit in English class," says Victor. "I wanted to tell you, but . . ."

I roll my eyes. I do remember him asking about extra credit, but whatever. He should have told me he was entering the contest.

"No, really. That one day you blew up at Sara, you were all like 'true friends don't stab each other in the back.' I was afraid you'd think I was doing the same thing."

"Well, aren't you?" I snap. "You ruined my *volcán de Fuego* and now you're trying to beat me at the Trailblazer contest."

"Don't be like that," Victor begs. "I'm not trying to sabotage you. You're my friend."

"No, I'm not. So just forget about talking to me ever again."

"I'm super sorry. I'm just doing the contest for the extra credit. I need to do well at Sendak to get into Bishop Crest. Remember?"

I stand and pick up my tray to go. He stands up too.

"You don't have to go. I'll go. That's your seat. I'll sit somewhere else," he says. I just want throw my chicken nuggets when he acts so sweet. "I know you have good reason to be mad, but I'm sorry. I wasn't trying to—"

"Whatever, Victor." I sit down. "I thought you were leaving?"

Victor gulps hard and looks shocked. I'm a little shocked myself. I want to click delete on those harsh words like a bad cell phone photo, but I can't. Victor walks away with his head down to sit with Diego and Ethan.

I really thought Victor was on my side. This whole time he was planning to compete against me just like Sara. Grace leans closer to me and taps me gently on the arm.

"Are you okay?" she asks.

I take a deep breath. "I wish this year would just end already. I'm so ready to say good-bye to Sendak."

Chapter 24

Nothing is going right for me this last year at Sendak. On top of everything at school, Bisa is still at the hospital. Adriana says I can't visit Bisabuelo feeling all sorry for myself, so I put on a happy face when we get off the elevator to Great-Gramp's floor and make sure that Secret is tucked away properly in my picnic basket.

Secret doesn't mind being snuck into the hospital. His name makes him perfect for escapades like this. He stays curled up and quiet in the bottom of the basket covered with a cloth napkin like he knows who we're going to visit.

Once I get to Bisa's room, Secret jumps out and leaps onto Great-Gramp's lap. Bisa's buddies from the GI Forum are there. They greet me and Adriana with waves and thumbs-up. I recognize all of them, except a few younger guys. Every shelf and counter space is covered with get-well cards, baskets of cookies, vases of flowers, and balloons.

Mr. Honig, one of my great-gramp's closest buddies, raises his can of soda to me. I smile back. "Allie, we were just talking about how your great-gramps and I met. Do you know that story?"

"Don't bore Allie with stories," Bisa says, and waves him off.

"I want to know. Tell me," I say. Mr. Honig has been in our life for as long as I've been alive, but I don't know how they met. "You know that when Rocky got out of the war, he opened a restaurant, right?"

A few of the other veterans nod and comment on how good the food was. Bisa's eyes light up, and Mr. Honig continues. "Your great-gramps had a sign on the door that said, 'Welcome home, soldiers. Please come in for a warm meal on us.'"

"I saw a picture of that in Bisa's scrapbook," I say excitedly. Bisa pats my hand.

"That's right, *mija*."

"I returned from Vietnam," Mr. Honig says, "and was having a hard time getting back into the swing of things . . . finding a job and whatnot. I was hitchhiking to Colorado across Kansas and I saw his sign. I had only a few bucks on me, but sure enough, your *bisa* welcomed me with a handshake and a delicious plate of carne asada."

It's hard for me to believe that Mr. Honig ever hitchhiked or had trouble finding a job. He owns his own construction company now.

"Were you homeless, Mr. Honig?" I ask.

"For a while, but then your great-gramps got me in with the veterans' center and they helped me get back on my feet."

"How many brothers did you feed, Rocky?" asks Auggie. "It's amazing you didn't go out of business."

Bisa lets out a chuckle. "Soldiers are too proud; they always left something. I never went broke, and they never went hungry."

"I didn't know about that," Adriana says. Bisa gives her a don't-worry-about-it wink.

"When I got back from the Gulf War, your great-gramps was there at the base," says Mr. Silva. "He welcomed all of us with big hugs. When he found out that me and a few other guys and gals didn't have any family to meet us, he took us out to dinner. True story. Your great-gramps is a kind man." Mr. Silva wipes his eyes, and I trade a smile with Bisa.

To this day, Bisa and Mr. Silva go to the nearest base a couple times a year to welcome troops home. They still buy soldiers with no family a dinner too, but Bisa always says that once the soldiers find out who he is they want to pay the check. My *bisa* never lets them.

"I have a true story to tell too," I say. "My fave story is about how you and your mom walked to a whole other town trying to get into school." Mr. Honig and Mr. Silva give me a knowing nod. "And now look"—I gesture to Adriana—"his great-granddaughter is going to Harvard."

Adriana gives Bisa and me a peck on the cheek.

"That's the best story of all," says Bisa.

I give Great-Gramps a tight hug. "I love you so much, Bisa," I say. "I'm so sorry I was angry about you not having the medal," I blurt out. "And I'm sorry that I didn't even want to take a picture of you without the medal. I didn't mean to make you stressed out and sick."

"*Mija*, you didn't make me sick," Bisa says and clears my bangs from my wet eyes. "I'm a *viejo*. Old guys like me get sick sometimes," he says, and pinches the tip of my nose. "I'm happy to help you with your project." Secret lies on his lap and purrs. I wipe my eyes and gaze around the room.

The room is filled with Bisa's friends. Where are mine? I should have been helping Victor with his project. After all, he only entered the contest for extra credit. He told me English was his toughest subject. And as for Sara, she was right to stop talking to me after the whole Furry Friend Photo Contest thing. She had lots of ideas about the photo contest, but I didn't think any of those ideas were good enough to win. Every idea she had, I rejected. Some friend I am.

For the first time I get what Bisa's been trying to tell me about how the best rewards are the ones that don't fit on a shelf. He may not have his Medal of Honor, but he has this room full of people who love him. People he calls friends and family. Why have I been so dense?

I grab my camera. Bisa winks at me like he knows what I'm thinking. "May I take a photo?" Bisa gathers everyone close to him. Secret sits up to be photographed too. Now, this is a photo that could have won the Furry Friend Photo Contest for sure!

"On a count of three," I say.

"Wait! Shouldn't you be in the photo, *mija*?" Bisa asks.

"Not this time." I shake my head and smile. "Say 'family'!"

Beep. Click. Flash. I've got my picture. The best picture of all.

When I get home from the hospital, I know exactly what I have to do. I log in to my Prezi account. I go through my entire presentation again. It's too much about war. It's not about Bisa. Secret paws each slide with disgust. When it's over, he even whips the screen with his tail.

"You're so right," I tell him. "What do you say, Secret? Are you ready for an all-nighter?"

ChapteR 25

I would like the auditorium to stop spinning. I look past Mrs. Wendy standing in front of me and see the theater swell with more and more people taking their seats.

"Alyssa, are you sure this is what you want to do?" She puts both of her hands on each of my shoulders like she needs to hold me up before she says anymore. "I know winning is important to you."

I don't flinch. "Yes," I nod to make my point. "I just thought you should know what I'm planning since you have to bring up my presentation for me."

"Okay, Alyssa," she says, and pats my arm. "I'm behind you all the way if this is what you want to do."

"Thank you." I give her a big hug, because when someone says they are behind me all the way, they deserve a hug. She leaves and the room spins some more.

Thankfully, Adriana, Ava, and Aiden show up.

"Adriana, I feel sick," I say. I grab hold of her hand and squeeze it. "I'm going to make a fool of myself."

"No you're not. Nerves are normal, Allie. Trust me. I know," she says.

"You get nervous too?"

"Right before every debate, I get these horrible stomach cramps," Adriana says. I can't believe what I'm hearing. She always seems so calm and confident at the debates.

"Everyone gets nervous, Allie," Aiden says. "It's normal. That's why I always have my headphones on before a game. I listen to music to calm me down."

"What? I thought you did that to look cool," I say. Aiden scoffs and shakes his head.

"Allie, do what I do before I perform onstage," chimes in Ava. "Spin around! And bam!" She whirls around and her pretty blue skirt swirls around her. "You turn the nervous energy on itself and convert it into star power!"

"Thanks, Ava, but please no more spinning," I beg. "The room. Everything is too much."

"Okay, ignore her. This is what you have to do," says Aiden. "See all those other kids out there?" He takes me by the shoulder and points out toward the crowd. "They don't have the courage to do what you're about to do, which is dominate the program. They are weak and—"

"Okay, thank you very much, Aiden," interrupts Adriana. "Not cool."

"That's what our coach tells us before every game." Aiden shrugs.

"Disturbing," says Adriana, and frowns. "Okay, you two go back to your seats. I'll get Allie through this."

Once they're gone, a stinging heat spreads across my scalp and over my entire body. I seriously regret wearing the purple jacket Ava picked out for me to go with my blue jeans and floral top. I whip off the jacket.

"I don't think I can do this," I say. I scan all the kids backstage with me, but I don't see Victor or Sara. Here I am ready to make a fool of myself in front of the world, and I don't have my two best friends, Sara and Victor, with me. Tonight is my chance to make everything right with them, my *bisa*, and just everything that's gone wrong this entire school year. If I'm going to win Sara and Victor back once and for all, I have to go big. Mount Everest big.

"Breathe with me, Allie. I have to admit, you're more nervous than I expected you to be. Are you sure everything is all right? Is there something else going on?"

I take a couple of deep breaths. She has no idea what I'm up to. No one does except for Secret and Mrs. Wendy. I know in my heart that I'm doing the right thing. I just hope that I don't lose my cool once they call me to present. I have one chance to make things right.

"Attention, everyone!" shouts a super-tall woman wearing a floor-length navy blue dress. "I'm Ms. Zaner and I will be hosting tonight's contest. Unless you're a finalist, we need you to take your seats now. We're about to begin."

"Okay, I've got to go. You'll be great. Keep breathing and look for us in the fifth row there. See Bisabuelo? Mom and Dad? Just focus on us, okay?" Adriana kisses me on the cheek. I don't want her to go. "You've got this, Allie."

Suddenly, she's gone. My stomach flip-flops some more. I look out toward the stage. It is set with a single microphone and eleven folding chairs. A large screen is pulled down to the side of the stage. The crowd backstage has thinned out. One guy is reading his poem out loud. As he practices, he uses his hands to set off each verse. I'm mesmerized by his performance.

"That's Clover Denton," says Sara, suddenly standing next to me. "He's from El Camino Charter School. They win every year. There are like four of them competing as finalists. Insane!"

I take a good look at Sara. She is all dressed up in a pretty red, white, and blue dress.

"I look dumb, right?" Sara asks when she notices me staring.

"You look very patriotic," I say.

"Thanks. I thought it wouldn't hurt."

"Where's your *familia*?" I ask.

"Same row as yours, see?"

I look out to the audience and spot Sara's parents next to my family. Since we were little, our families have always hung out together. After tonight, I wonder if everything can go back to the way it was with Sara and me. I hope so.

It was a bad idea to look at the crowd again. More families are spilling in, and I feel hotter. "Don't let me do that again. Seeing all those people is too much."

"My mom said to look at her when I'm onstage, but no way. That will just freak me out. My plan is to sing to that light at the back of the auditorium."

It feels good to be talking to Sara like this. "Have you seen Victor?" I ask. "I'd really like to talk to both of you about something important."

"He's back here somewhere. Adriana was talking to him on her way out," she says. "He's like, crazy nervous. But I think you'll have to wait, the event is about to start."

Just then a voice booms over the speakers, "Ladies and gentleman, welcome to this year's Trailblazer contest. Please meet this year's finalists." My throat tightens up and my chest hurts. I feel bad that Victor is nervous. I wish I could tell him that I wish him the best.

"Students!" Ms. Zaner calls out. "It's time to take our seats onstage. Let's go."

Sara and I line up with the rest of the finalists and follow Ms. Zaner out onto the stage.

While the audience applauds, we take our seats. Once we've all sat down, cameras flash at us from the audience. I spot my *bisabuelo* and give him a small wave. He waves back.

I can do this. I have to do this. This is my chance.

Ms. Zaner introduces all of us one by one. Victor is in the very last seat of our row. When she calls his name, I clap extra hard and hope he notices. The three judges are seated in the front row with tablets in their hands.

After a few instructions to the audience about turning off cell phones, cameras, and being silent during our presentations, Ms. Zaner says we'll go in alphabetical order. With a name like Velasco, this means I'm dead last. Why couldn't we go by first names? Then I'd be first to read and get this all over with.

Clover Denton is the first to present. He removes the microphone from the stand and flashes a huge smile at the crowd. He tells everyone that this isn't the type of poetry that they have to sit quietly through with their hands folded on their laps. He says if they feel like snapping or clapping while he's reading his poem "it's totally cool" with him. Then he jumps right into his poem about a famous Brazilian soccer player. His poem isn't like the poetry we study at Sendak. It's more like a rap song, and there are times when the audience laughs or claps at something they hear. Now *this* is the kind of poetry I could listen to all day!

Sara taps my hand. "He's really good," she whispers.

Clover ends his poem with a bow, and everyone gets up on their feet and cheers. I swallow hard. Standing ovation. This is going to be a fiasco for me.

After two photography presentations, we finally get to the *G*s. Victor walks up to the microphone. I'm nervous for him. My whole body starts to tremble again. He's dressed in blue jeans with an eagle belt buckle and a white dress shirt. He looks cute. If he is nervous, it doesn't show. He clears his throat.

"I wrote this poem for my dad because he is a trailblazer," Victor starts. His voice is calm and warm. "My dad, Gustavo Garcia, came here from Mexico to make a better life for us. Because of him, I get to go to a nice school and I'll be the first to graduate from college someday. My poem is titled 'A Poem for My Father.'

"My father doesn't need this poem,
Instead he could use a new truck.
Our truck never works on cold days and that is when
My father walks miles to work in black boots with worn
   soles.

"My father doesn't need this poem,
Instead he could use new shoes.
His feet are always red and blistered,
By the end of a long workday.

"My father doesn't need this poem.
It won't fix his truck, buy him new shoes,
Or pay for my expensive school,

"But I write it for him anyway
Because I love him,
Because I want him to know
I'm grateful."

Wow, Victor. Along with the audience, I clap. His poem is awesome. I had no idea he had it in him to write poetry. His father wipes away tears while holding one of Victor's littlest sisters in his arms. I hate the lump that's forming in my throat. I need to be able to speak when it's my turn. I need to be able to make things right.

Sara leans over to me. "Did you know Victor could write like that?"

"No clue," I say. "I've been clueless about a lot of things lately." Sara gives me a surprised look but doesn't say anything else. As Victor walks back to his seat, he doesn't even look my direction. I'm so mad at myself. Victor just wants a scholarship to get into Bishop Crest so he can go to a good high school and college to help his family. He wants his chance to be a trailblazer, a piñata buster for his family. And all I've been obsessed with is winning something shiny for my trophy shelf. How did he put up with me?

It's finally Sara's turn. She starts with a few words about my *bisabuelo*.

"This song is dedicated to Rocky Velasco, World War II veteran and recipient of the Congressional Medal of Honor . . ." she says. "He is here with us tonight. Bisabuelo, would you please stand?"

My *bisabuelo* slowly stands up. The crowd gets on its feet to applaud. He waves and says thank you to everyone. The applause is louder than thunder. Sara takes a seat on the stool with her guitar. She begins to thrum a few chords while the applause fades. She recites her song from pure memory. Clover Denton starts clapping along and eggs on all of us to clap along too. When she's done, her dad kisses her mom. They're beaming with pride. Bisa gives her a thumbs-up.

"Good job, Sara," I say when she sits down. Sara loves and cares for my *bisa*. And I've done nothing but punish her for wanting to write a song about him. I should have been happy that someone else wanted to honor my great-gramps. I could have helped her and that could have been the thing that brought us together. Instead I let it split us farther apart.

All this time, I thought I was being Junko Tabei, climbing my Mount Everest, but instead I've been a big wet, soppy avalanche trying to bring down both Sara and Victor.

Next is Skyler St. John from El Camino Charter. Why does every El Camino student have a cool name? Skyler sings a song about a teacher who died from breast cancer last year.

184

The song is sweet and honest. It's as if she shared a page straight from her diary.

After a few more Prezi presentations, poems, and songs about moms, dads, teachers, and famous athletes, Ms. Zaner calls my name. I feel a sudden urge to bolt for the exit doors, but I walk up to the microphone. I find Bisabuelo in the audience.

Mrs. Wendy gives me an "are-you-sure" look. I am. I turn back to the screen and see my presentation appear. I take a deep breath and lean into the microphone. I wish my knees would stop trembling.

"I had it all wrong," I start. My voice is shaky, but I keep going. "The presentation I submitted earlier to the judges focused on the wrong things. And even though I know I will be disqualified, I want to make it right this evening by sharing a brand-new presentation."

My family looks back and forth at each other, confused. Bisabuelo tips his hat to me, and my legs stop trembling. I feel like I've found my magic pickax and I'm ready to climb this mountain. I've got this.

All my nerves float away when I see the first photograph up on the screen. It's the black-and-white photo of my *bisabuelo*, his mom, and his brother.

"This is where everything started for Rocky Velasco.

He's the little boy in this photo with a closed-mouth smile." The next slide zooms in on Bisa's face. "Trailblazers start out as regular kids, just like the ten of us here on this stage. We don't know where the future will lead us, but at some point, like with my great-gramps, we'll be confronted with challenges and opportunities. It's what we do with those challenges and opportunities that define us."

The next slide is a school class picture of Bisabuelo. He is maybe ten years old in this photo. He's off to the left of the picture, as if he wasn't allowed to stand with the rest of the class. "For my *bisabuelo*, being poor and unable to speak English, he faced more challenges than I ever will, but he never gave up no matter how tough life was, because he was focused on making life better for his future family. Even though I didn't exist yet, my *bisa* was already thinking of me, my family, and our dreams."

I click and his army photo appears. "When the United States of America declared war on Japan after Pearl Harbor, my *bisabuelo*, at the young age of seventeen, volunteered. By the time the war ended, he was awarded the prestigious Congressional Medal of Honor for valor in action. He is the last living World War II Medal of Honor recipient in our state and one of the last few in our country. But what's most important is that after the war, my *bisa* found his calling in life." Several of the photos I took of my *bisa* at the GI Forum shoot across the screen. "For the rest of his life, he would dedicate himself to helping other veterans of war.

"How do you recognize a true trailblazer?" I ask the audience. "Is it by the medals they wear?" The slides stop, and the image of Bisa with the empty medal box zooms in slowly. I love how Bisa's eyes glisten in the photo. The judges are now smiling and nodding at me. "Is it by the trophies they win?"

I pause and let the question float over everyone in the theater. I click for the final photograph. The image of Great-Gramps and all of his friends and family around him at the hospital comes into view. "You can always tell who a true trailblazer is by the friends and family that surround them. True trailblazers are motivated not by glory, but for love. For love of family, friends, and country. Their lives and stories remind us that we too can be great and accomplish the impossible. My great-gramps, Rocky Velasco, inspires me to be better everyday. Thank you very much."

Applause sweeps though the theater. Next thing I know the judges are standing and soon the entire audience is up on their feet too. Are they standing for me? For Bisa? It doesn't matter.

As I take my seat, I steal a glance at Victor. He's clapping too, but he doesn't look up at me. Sara and Skyler both pat me on the back and say my presentation was amazing.

I have to admit, I feel great.

Ms. Zaner tells the audience to give all the finalists another round of applause. "We'll take an intermission and be back in twenty minutes with the results. Who will be this year's winner? Stick around and see!"

ChAPTER 26

At break, Ms. Zaner comes over to me and tells me that I am disqualified for submitting a new presentation. She says sorry a hundred times. "Your presentation gave me goose bumps," she says.

I'm allowed to stay on the stage, but there will be no points for me. I will not win this contest. This news should hurt, but it doesn't. In fact, I can't stop smiling. From their seats, my parents are blowing me kisses, giving me the thumbs-up. Bisabuelo smiles. Just smiles.

Sara looks at me for a long time. "How are you not upset that you've just been disqualified?"

"Oh yeah, I expected that. I changed my presentation. They had to."

"You sabotaged yourself?" Sara shakes her head. "Who are you? Where is Allie Velasco?"

I laugh and feel all the nerves of the past two weeks fade. Now, I just need to fix things with Sara and Victor once and for all.

"I'm really proud of you, Allie," she says. "It took guts to do what you did. I watched Bisa's face as you were presenting. He was loving it. Did you see?"

"Yes," I say, and look down at my shoes. "I had to do it. I just wish I had learned earlier that winning isn't worth ruining friendships. Maybe if I had, I wouldn't have totally messed up with you and Victor."

Sara turns to me with a shocked expression.

"You haven't *totally* messed up with me." Sara plays with a bracelet on her wrist. "And . . . I'm not talking to Hayley anymore. She's mean."

"You're just now figuring that out? What did you ever see in her in the first place?"

"She was fun. You were too obsessed with winning medals and living up to your Velasco family legacy or whatever.

The final straw was over winter break when we were sup-posed to do the Furry Friends Photo Contest together and you turned all crazy. There's no talking to you when you're trying to win something."

I gulp hard. I've been a crazed Chihuahua. It's like what happened with Victor and the Trailblazer contest. "I'm sorry, Sara." I shake my head slowly.

"I prefer this new Allie, the one who redid her project knowing she would be disqualified."

"I prefer the new Allie too," I say softly. "But I miss the old Sara. Do you think we could be best friends again like we used to be?"

Sara starts to scrape the polish off of her thumbnail, but doesn't answer.

I gently tap her hands. "Stop it."

"Thanks." She frowns and then pulls off a turquoise-and-purple bracelet from her wrist. "This is for you. You stopped wearing your friendship bracelet after the April Fool's disaster, so I made you a new one last night. Like it?"

I quickly put it on. "Thanks. And what about Hayley?"

She shrugs. "We were never that close. She and Sophie are closer friends. I was just hanging out with her because I needed a break from your hyperobsessed—"

"Crazy Chihuahua-ness," I finish for her. She covers a

giggle with her hands. "Hey, do you want to join us for tacos after?"

"Definitely." She smiles. "Meeting the new Allie has made me super hungry."

The auditorium lights switch off and on. "Here we go," I say.

Families who went out to get punch and cookies from the lobby rush back into the auditorium. Ms. Zaner comes out from backstage waving an envelope over her head. "We have a winner!"

"Would all ten finalists please stand?"

"Good luck, Sara," I whisper.

All ten of us stand up. I look over at Victor, hoping to catch his eye, but he never looks my way.

"I will ask the top three finalists to step forward and then announce this year's winner of the Trailblazer contest," Ms. Zaner says. I cross my fingers for Sara and Victor to be in the top three. Please let it be someone from Sendak Elementary this year. Please. Please. Please.

Mrs. Zaner takes a deep gasp for breath over the microphone. "Clover Denton, Skyler St. John, and Victor Garcia please step forward."

The crowd erupts into cheers. I nudge Sara.

"I'm glad it's Victor," she says.

"Now for this year's winner of the Kansas Trailblazer Contest," says Ms. Zaner. She opens the envelope. "Victor Garcia from Sendak Elementary! You are this year's winner!" The audience roars.

At the center of the stage, Victor accepts his check and trophy from Ms. Zaner and shakes hands with the judges. All the other finalists encircle him to congratulate him, but I can't move. "This is a first win for Sendak Elementary!" Ms. Zaner announces into the microphone.

Sara tugs on my jacket, "Let's go congratulate him."

I freeze. "I don't think he'll want to see me," I say as Victor rushes off to his family at the edge of the stage. I'm so happy for him. Too happy to want to bother him with my apology when he should be happy and celebrating. "Can you tell him that I want to talk to him though?" Sara nods and rushes off. I veer toward my family, who are waiting for me in the audience.

My mom and dad are the first to reach me and give me a hug.

"Like the song goes, you took my breath away," Dad says.

Adriana kisses me. "You had everyone completely enraptured. Did it feel good, Allie?"

I nod. It did. Aiden gives me a pat on the back and tells me, "Super proud of you, sis."

Ava hugs me and says, "You showed real star power."

"Allie . . ." Bisa pulls me into a hug. "I'm so proud of you." I let myself stay wrapped up in his hug. I never want to let go of Bisa. It was only a week ago that we were all in the hospital fearing the worst. And now here he is with all of us. I feel so lucky. When I finally let go, I look for Victor, but I don't see him anywhere.

As I head out of the auditorium with my family, I keep looking for him.

"Sara, did you tell Victor I wanted to talk to him?" I ask. She nods. "What did he say?"

"He didn't say anything. He waited around for a little while, but after a few minutes, he left with his family."

"Oh, I was hoping to apologize and see if wanted to join us for tacos too . . . I guess I messed up, again."

"Don't stress about it, Allie," she says. "You guys will work it out."

For once in a long time, everything in my world feels right. Bisabuelo is back home. Sara and I are friends again. Aiden and Ava seem genuinely proud of me even though I didn't win first place. The only thing missing from my happiness is Victor. Will he forgive me or is it too late?

Chapter 27

On the ride to Cosmic Taco, Sara says Clover and Skyler have also been accepted to Bishop Crest Middle, which is awesome. I can't wait to head to Bishop Crest next year with Sara and new friends like Clover and Skyler. Still, what about Victor? Will he get into Bishop Crest? Will he get the scholarship he needs to afford it? I hope that him winning this contest tonight will help.

We arrive at Cosmic Taco and pile out of the car. I breathe in the fresh April air mixed with the scent of spicy chili coming from the restaurant. Last time we were here, I had lost the science fair. This time, I've lost again, but it doesn't feel the same.

That's when I see a boy leaning against the front of the restaurant. He looks up, sees me, and heads my direction.

"What is Victor doing here? How did he know I'd be here?" I ask Sara.

"Um, I might have texted him and told him where we were going." Sara shrugs. "You said you wanted to talk to him. Here's your chance."

My heart does a cartwheel. I meet Victor halfway. I'm not sure if he'll accept a hug, so I put out my hand for an awkward handshake. He grins and takes it.

"Congrats, Victor!" I say. My family comes over and give him hugs and congratulations.

"We're all happy you won, Victor," says Adriana. "Your poem was beautiful."

"*Gracias*. I'm glad it's over. It was nerve-racking. There were so many people staring at me," he says. He sneaks a shy look over at me, and I smile back. Something is definitely on his mind. Maybe he's waiting for my apology?

Here it goes. In front of Bisa, Sara, and the whole family. If I can speak in front of an auditorium of people, I can do this.

"Victor, I need to talk to you—"

"Actually, I'd like to say something," interrupts Victor. "Can I go first, Allie?"

"Okay, I guess," I say, and chop down on my bottom lip. Maybe he's going to complain about me or tell everyone what a dork I've been. He'd be right, but still . . .

"A couple of days ago, I was told a secret about you, and I want to share it with everyone."

"Yes! A secret!" Ava squeals. "Tell us!" I roll my eyes at her because she is always little Miss Drama. Adriana puts her in sisterly head lock.

A secret? I gulp hard. Does he have to tell everyone? I may pass out. I narrow my eyes at him.

"Adriana told me about something you did," Victor continues. I look over at Adriana. What could she have told him? Adriana winks at me like everything is okay. Whatever Victor has to say I can take it. My face, head, and entire body feels hot again, like I'm standing onstage.

"Stop stalling! Let's hear it already!" Aiden says.

Thanks a lot, Aiden.

"Adriana told me that you asked her to write a recommendation letter for me to help me get into Bishop Crest. True or false, Allie?"

"True." I nod. Sara gives me a that's-cool nudge, but I'm still nervous about what else Victor is getting at.

"Well, I've been accepted to Bishop Crest and I won a It Takes a Village scholarship, so I'll be with both of you next year," says Victor, pointing at me and Sara.

My heart jumps. Yay! I clap with everyone else. I'm so happy for him. Now Victor and I will be in middle school together. Victor smiles at me. I let out a sigh of relief. I thought he was going to tell everyone that I was an over-competitive Miss Prissy-Pants.

Victor looks straight at me now with warm twinkling brown eyes. I've never noticed before how much his eyes shine like a hundred trophies. "Thank you for believing in me enough to ask Adriana to write a letter. That, to me, is the real prize tonight."

"Yes, it is," says Bisa, and he kisses the top of my head. "Let's leave these kids alone with their crazy secrets and get some tacos." Everyone heads toward the restaurant, but I chase after Bisa.

"I love you." I hug him super tight. "I wanted to do the right thing tonight and tell your story."

"*Te quiero mucho,* Allie. I'll see you inside for victory tacos." He walks into the restaurant, leaving me outside with Sara and Victor.

"You said you had something to tell me?" says Victor.

"That's right. I wanted to say I'm sorry for being such a trailblazing dork about the whole contest, Victor. I'm really sorry about being mean to you," I say. "You too, Sara. I can't say I'm sorry enough."

"If you say you're sorry again, I'm taking back my bracelet," says Sara. "Last time, okay?"

Victor shakes his head. "You go a little overboard, Allie, but that's what I like about you." Victor digs into his front pocket and pulls out a red ribbon with some sort of tin lid attached to it. "This is for you. It's not a fancy trophy, but I want you to have it because you believed in me and helped me get into Bishop Crest."

Victor gives me the handmade medal. I quickly put it on. It says *#1 Best Friend*.

"My brothers and sisters helped me make it last night," he says. "I've been planning to give it to you ever since Adriana told me about what you did."

"I love it," I say, and show it off to Sara.

"You got your very own medal, Allie," says Sara.

I lock eyes with Victor. "Thank you." I give him a great big hug and can't help but giggle when he hugs me back. It's so much better than our awkward handshake earlier. I know that medals aren't the most important thing in the world, but when you get one for being a #1 Best Friend . . . well, that feels like being Billy Mills crossing the finish line, Gwendolyn Brooks taking home the Pulitzer Prize, and Junko Tabei reaching the top of Mount Everest—all at the same time.

ACKNOWLEDGMENTS

I would like to give the following wonderful individuals a huge shiny gold trophy for supporting me as I completed this second novel. As always, big hug to my agent, Adriana Dominguez, for her encouragement and believing in my voice. You're #1!

Thank you a hundred times to my editor, Anna Bloom, for the amazing revisions, enthusiasm, and laughs.

Muchas gracias to Rocky R., World War II veteran, for sharing your scrapbook with me. You're an inspiration to me and I thank you for your service to our country.

A big kiss and *#1 Best Friend* medal to my husband for keeping me sane and fully supplied with snacks while I wrote this second novel.

Finally, special thanks to all the teachers, librarians, and kids who've invited me to speak at their schools. Getting to know all of you has been the best part of this entire writing journey. I hope I've made you proud with this second book.